Sex & Taipei City

Sex & Taipei City

stories

Yu-Han Chao

Red Hen Press | *Pasadena, CA*

Book design by Mark E. Cull

Library of Congress Cataloging-in-Publication Data

Names: Chao, Yu-Han, 1981– author.
Title: Sex & Taipei City : stories / Yu-Han Chao.
Other titles: Sex and Taipei City
Description: Pasadena, CA : Red Hen Press, [2019]
Identifiers: LCCN 2018042731 | ISBN 9781597090438
Classification: LCC PS3603.H3584 A6 2019 | DDC 813/.6—dc23
LC record available at https://lccn.loc.gov/2018042731

The National Endowment for the Arts, the Los Angeles County Arts
Commission, the Ahmanson Foundation, the Dwight Stuart Youth
Fund, the Max Factor Family Foundation, the Pasadena Tournament of
Roses Foundation, the Pasadena Arts & Culture Commission and the
City of Pasadena Cultural Affairs Division, the City of Los Angeles De-
partment of Cultural Affairs, the Audrey & Sydney Irmas Charitable
Foundation, the Kinder Morgan Foundation, the Allergan Foundation,
and the Riordan Foundation partially support Red Hen Press.

First Edition
Published by Red Hen Press
www.redhen.org

Acknowledgments

Thank you to my mentors, William J. Cobb, Charlotte Holmes, and Josip Novakovich.

With family, anything is possible. All my love to the Chao family, Chen family, Juarez family, Lin family, and Shu family.

Friends and community are everything. Many amazing people have been there with me through it all—writers, artists, teachers, students—everyone from Taiwan to Pennsylvania to Vermont to California. Thank you.

Many thanks to journals that gave these stories a home: *Amoskeag*: "Cat Spring Roll"; *Diverse Voices Quarterly*: "Immersion"; *Eastlit*: "Mine," "Rainy Night Stand Up"; *The Externalist*: "Crisp Skin Thick Soup"; *The Evening Street Review*: "My Strange Grandpa"; *J Journal*: "Writing on the Basement Wall"; *Motherverse*: "Betel Nut Beauty"; *Melusine*: "Daughter"; *Sphere*: "Simple As That"; *Storyscape Journal*: "Seven Pieces at a Time"; *Timber Creek Review*: "Passport Baby"; *Wisconsin Review*: "Yuan Zu Socializing"; *Zyzzyva*: "The Strange Objects Museum."

In memory of my mother

Contents

The Strange Objects Museum

CHEN'S FAMILY HAD, for generations, sold food—various kinds, in various forms, from ruby-like candied fruit to char-grilled squid and fresh noodle soup. But Chen wanted to try his luck with something new.

His small town where the Danshui River met the sea had been transformed first by the war, then by all the new factories and their pollution, and then, after the light rail had been run out from Taipei, by tourists, drawn by the gilded Buddhist temple at the top of the hill.

When he got married, Chen used the red-envelope money to open a bike store—he'd worked in one since he was a teenager and felt comfortable with basic machinery. He also liked helping people with their transportation needs. But for some time, business had been declining—people simply didn't use bicycles as much anymore. He had no bright idea of his own, but everyone else in the neighborhood was aiming for the tourist market, and that made sense to him, too.

His friend, Dow, whom he had known from elementary school, had an antique store, an eclectic assortment of erotic manuscripts, artwork, and playthings . . . as well as a few ancient torture devices. These objects drew more curious people into the antique store, whispering and pointing, than real customers or collectors. Dow suggested that Chen take a few items from his inventory, at a low price, and set up a Strange Objects Museum.

The first item Dow showed Chen was a Ming Dynasty chastity belt that looked like a sumo wrestler's dusty loincloth.

"You can let your customers try it on," Dow said with a laugh. "People love that—when you let them touch things or try them on."

Chen's lips curled into a nervous smile. Dow was always the one boy trying to peek under girls' skirts when they were in elementary school together; Chen did not entirely trust his friend's judgment in terms of people or business. Chen had been brought up in a traditional and conservative family—he even felt relieved when his eccentric father-in-law died, because the old man, who was not at all conservative, watched the Japanese porn channel at too high a volume.

"I'll lend the chastity belt to you for your first month," Dow said. "If it does well, then you buy it from me. If not, then I'll just take it back. What do you think?"

"That's very generous of you," Chen said.

At least it was a chastity belt, which promoted chasteness—nothing obscene. Besides, like many Taiwanese, Chen could never resist something free.

"That's settled then." Dow nodded, satisfied.

In fact, Dow was a smart businessman: he knew that once one offered a free sample to a customer, the customer would be more likely to buy something else. Most successful business owners, from department store managers to night market vendors, knew this trick. Dow guided his friend to his storage room and pointed at a dragon-shaped basin.

"This is a scientific item, also very good, because your customers can have hands-on experience with it. You put water in the basin and have them rub the sides with their palms. The friction makes water drops spring up at the edges. Let me show you."

Dow emptied a mineral water bottle into the basin, set it on a dusty desk, and wet his hands in the water. He rubbed his palms together, then slowly placed them on the brass handles of the basin. He rubbed back and forth, increasing the speed. Little water droplets sprang up from the sides, just as he'd said.

"That's brilliant," Chen said. "Is that a trick?"

"Absolutely not. Anybody can do it. You try."

Chen copied Dow's movements. He rubbed and rubbed until his hands ached, but the water did not respond. A few eddies moved across the surface of the water, but no drops sprang from the surface as they had when Dow demonstrated.

Chen frowned. "I don't think I'm making it work."

"I'll tell you what. I'll loan you this as well, for a month, at no cost."

"Oh, that's really too nice of you, but I'm afraid I can't accept."

"Nonsense. What are friends for? Consider it my way of showing my support for your new venture. Let me show you one last thing. I guarantee it will draw a crowd."

Dow grinned as he moved some cardboard boxes out of the way and removed a gray piece of cloth to reveal something at the bottom of a deep wooden box. It looked like a saddle with a stick-like object standing up from the center. Chen gasped. The stick-like object was a penis.

"This . . . this . . . is quite, em, interesting."

"Of course it's interesting. Haven't you heard of the Ten Cruelest Tortures of the Ching Dynasty? This is one of them! You take an adulteress—or an immoral woman of any flavor—and sit her on this saddle, naked, with her you-know-what stretched by this stick here. Then you parade her through the streets. The Ching were really creative with their punishments, weren't they? Just imagine."

Chen tried hard not to imagine. The penis-shaped part was about seven inches tall and two inches in diameter. He knew this could become a true attraction for his Strange Objects Museum. In their Unbelievable But True Shop, his neighbors had a two-headed tortoise, a dried fish with a human face, Siamese twins in a jar, live parrots, and a transgender performer who showed up every other week and sang traditional Taiwanese opera. To top his neighbor's curiosities, this saddle was essential.

"I'll buy this piece," Chen said, a little more quickly than he'd intended.

"Good man. Who would have thought a square like you would buy something like this? Mind you, keep your young daughter off of this. Once she's had a taste of it, she'll never be content with a regular man."

Chen was reluctant to wager his entire economic future on his new business, so, although he sold off his most recent inventory at half price, he planned to continue doing repairs. Meanwhile, he converted his storefront into a museum within one hectic month.

Since his daughter, Sheri, had been idling around all day since she'd begun taking business classes in the evening at the local vocational school, Chen put her behind a counter to sell tickets. Nailed to the wall behind her was a large mirror with a sign: IF YOU CAN LICK YOUR NOSE WITH YOUR TONGUE, ENTRANCE IS FREE.

Many people tried to lick the tips of their noses before this mirror, but so far, only one customer could actually do it. Sheri took a Polaroid of him and let him in for free.

As the weeks passed, the Strange Objects Museum did well, and Chen purchased the antiques that Dow had loaned him—at rather high prices. Sheri grew used to the sight of the penis-saddle and the visitors' amusement with it. Dow suggested putting a sign in front of the penis-saddle: PLEASE TRY SITTING ON. And another by the chastity belt: PLEASE TRY ON. Chen did so.

Female visitors often challenged one another to fit their legs into the chastity belt. The men seemed less willing to touch the belt, probably because, generally, Taiwanese felt that men should not remain virgins, while women should. No one ever tried to sit on the saddle; everyone considered the invitation a rather pathetic joke.

One rainy afternoon, a tall young woman with shampoo-commercial hair and long legs in short shorts came to the museum with her friend, both of them sucking on ruby-red, jewel-like sticks of candied baby tomatoes. Sheri was sure the tall girl was an ABC, American Born Chinese, because of her distinctly un-Taiwanese makeup—all eyeliner and bronzer. Both of them looked about college age.

They stopped in front of the penis-saddle.

"Oh my god." The Taiwanese girl giggled.

"This is nice," the ABC laughed. She studied the penis portion of the saddle for some time. "It's not very big, though."

The Taiwanese girl giggled even more.

"Honestly, it's not. But actually, I would totally like to have one of these myself. What a good idea. Something you can just ride—"

Her friend interrupted her, "Shhh, this is Taiwan. You shouldn't talk like that."

"Why not? It's true. I've never had a boyfriend with a dick that thin and puny. I'll bet that wasn't torture, the women were totally enjoying their rides on these saddles."

"You are incorrigible," the Taiwanese girl said, pushing her friend. "Stop showing off."

The ABC shrugged. "I'm just saying, I'd like one of these at home. I do believe I'd enjoy that very, *very* much."

Sheri pretended that she wasn't listening to the conversation, but the ABC's words struck her. A virgin herself, Sheri had considered this sculpted penis quite magnificent; she expected everyone to think of this saddle as a torture device, a source of great pain. Now that its size had been dismissed by an ABC with long hair and short shorts, Sheri did not know what to think.

The ABC and her friend played with the dragon-shaped basin for a while and left without bothering with the rest of the museum.

Tossing and turning in her bed that night, Sheri dreamed of the Mighty Cock on the saddle. Just as she was about to lower herself onto it, however, she woke up. She tried to go back to sleep—to continue the rather intriguing dream— but could not.

She looked at the clock on her night stand: 2:35 a.m. She could hear her father snoring in his bedroom. She got up to use the bathroom and passed the back hallway that led to the Strange Objects Museum. She was still thinking about her dream. What harm would it do to try out the saddle? She pulled aside the curtain that separated her home from the museum. There it was, the Mighty Cock, seemingly beckoning to her underneath a dark red piece of cloth.

Sheri approached it and lifted the cloth. She touched the tip of the cock. It was surprisingly cold, hard, and smooth. She pulled the heavy saddle up into her arms and set it on the floor. Looking about her one more time out of innate shame, Sheri tugged at her panties and pulled them down, almost tripping as she lifted her right leg. Then she lowered herself, letting the brass cock just touch her. She felt resistance, as if there was a wall inside her. She tried to sit down farther, but the cock felt too cold and strange. It clearly did not fit, and she felt ridiculous. Not tonight. She picked up her panties and pulled them back on.

She walked to the bathroom to inspect herself. The cock had not done any damage.

The next night, Sheri could hardly wait until everyone was asleep. This time, she warmed the cock first with her hands. When she lowered herself upon it, she shifted her lower body left and right and moved her labia with her fingers. She sat down deeper and deeper, but again felt resistance. A shooting pain forced her to stop.

The following night, Sheri was prepared for the pain. She moved herself cautiously and gently, so the pain came slow, like an intense soreness that traveled to her stomach and made her ill. For a while, she no longer wanted to sit down all the way on the saddle; she just wanted the feeling to stop. But she couldn't stop now, not when she had already split her hymen with this torture device for immoral women. She sucked her lips in and forced herself down lower than ever before.

She was all the way down now. The metal cock felt cool and hard inside her.

She smiled to herself. She was no longer a virgin.

She tentatively lifted and lowered her body. Her breath quickened; her heart beat faster. Her right index finger found her clitoris, and the heat within her triggered a long, trembling explosion.

Everything around her looked different afterward. It was like she had crossed over some kind of watershed. She returned the cock and covered it with its cloth. Then she walked down the hallway, back to her bedroom, with a smile on her face.

Sheri felt extremely glad her father had ditched the bicycle shop and opened the Strange Objects Museum.

Flower Girl

WHEN BAY SHUFFLED into the living room in mismatched slippers, book in hand, her mother looked up from the thousand dollar bills she was counting for a red envelope.

"Aren't you excited you got picked to be flower girl at your cousin's wedding?"

"No." Bay pulled a long face. "I'm in fifth grade already. I'm too old to be a flower girl. That's baby stuff."

"But you're so petite, perfect for a flower girl. You should be happy your cousin invited you. His fiancée is a kindergarten teacher, and I'm sure she has no shortage of flower girls if she wants them, you know."

"Then she should just ask them, not me." Bay hated it when her mother mentioned her size. She was always the last one when the class lined up by height and perpetually seated in the front row so overexcited teachers' spit landed on the open pages of her textbook.

Her mother's enthusiasm was indefatigable. "Come, dear, don't be a grouch. You're going to have a beautiful new dress for the occasion. Wouldn't you like that?"

"Maybe." Bay's heart leapt at the prospect of a new dress. Her mother made her wear the same old, frilly thing to Sunday school so often that the other girls made fun of her. She knew it was shallow and probably a sin to be vain at church, like the little girl with red shoes who danced herself to death. All the same, during individual prayer time, when she looked down at the frills in her lap, she could not help folding her hands tight and asking God for a new dress.

After dinner, Bay lingered in the hallway, eavesdropping on her father and mother in the living room. She was curious about this male cousin who was marrying—she hardly ever heard anything about her father's sister's part of the family, as she had married a "bad husband" who wouldn't let her come home for Chinese New Year. "So this kindergarten teacher is pregnant, I hear," Bay's mother said, lowering her voice as she uttered the word *pregnant*.

"Ay. That boy has caused my older sister so much trouble. He never studied in school, lost just about every job he's had, and now he's gone and knocked up a girl."

"Aiyah, at least he's willing to do the right thing. So many marriages nowadays are *Get on the bus now and pay the fare later*, anyway."

"He thinks life is all games, although he is already thirty." Bay's father made a *tsk tsk* sound against his teeth.

"Well, your own brother was no better, half a *jing* to eight *liang*, wasn't he? That's why he got married in the first place, because his daughter, Shia, was already in the oven."

"My brother wasn't that bad, at least he always had a stable job. And things worked out for them. Shia is all grown up and has a good job now."

"And may she find a husband, poor girl, always being set up by her parents with these slow, earnest country boys." Bay's mother, born and bred in Taipei, thought of her husband's southern Taiwanese family and their tastes as "country."

"What do you mean *country boys*?" Bay's father sounded irked.

"Oh, I don't mean you, of course. It's just that I've heard your family keeps setting Shia up with these dopes who don't know how to talk and dress like bumpkins. And they think government jobs are like an iron bowl, the best thing under the sun."

"What's wrong with a government job? It's steady pay and guaranteed retirement."

"I'm just saying they're very old fashioned," Bay's mother said softly.

Bay's parents cherished each other enough; they married late and had taken even longer to procreate. For the first five years of their marriage, Bay's mother put up with a great deal of jeering from her parents-in-law, who said she "couldn't pop out a child—even a pig can do that." Bay knew her mother held a grudge.

The wedding rehearsal took place the day before the cere-mony so the bride and groom could rent their tux and gown for two days in a row at a discount. Strands of white chiffon lay in the pews, waiting to be attached to the ceiling and the walls. In the background, a janitor with a slight hunch pushed an industrial-strength vacuum before him. Squeal-ing children ran about, playing tag.

Bay's new dress was a scratchy tea-length gown with many layers of stiff tulle and little bowtie accents. It was probably a bit much for Sunday school, but Bay secretly en-joyed the poofiness of the skirt and she didn't want to act ungrateful. *Thank you, God, for my new dress*, she prayed. Anyway, there were no girls her age around to make fun of her. The ring-bearer was barely potty-trained and had to be rushed to the bathroom after an accident. He also had diffi-culty walking down the aisle, beelining to his mother every time instead.

"Okay, let's try this again," said the wedding organizer, a middle-aged man with weary bags under his eyes. He squinted into the microphone as he spoke. "Walk toward the groom, kid—see the groom? Groom, wave to the ring-bearer, please. Thank you. Now, walk to that nice man and give him the pillow with the ring, kiddo."

The wedding organizer wiped his brow with the back of his hand and mumbled something about children making or breaking the ceremony.

After the rehearsal, the adults moved their conversation to a coffee house across from the church, and Bay slinked onto the sidewalk outside. She spotted the groom in the garden next to the coffee house, talking on his cell phone. She ran past him into the street, dodged a bicycle, and entered the church.

Inside, the bride, a sallow-faced young woman with thick-framed glasses and long hair tied into a thin ponytail, sat on the steps beside the altar, blowing up pink and white balloons and securing them with knots. The bride's face sagged behind the frames, and her eyes looked red, perhaps the effect of blowing up too many balloons. Bay watched this scene from the doorway of the church, feeling sorry for her. They couldn't afford a helium tank for her wedding? Why wasn't the groom helping?

The groom still had his phone pressed against his ear when Bay left the church to look for him. Waiting for several scooters with families of three or four on them to zoom by before she crossed the street, Bay watched her cousin. Tall Korean grass, punctuated with trumpet-like daffodils, swayed in the breeze. As she got close enough to hear his words, however, they ruined the picturesque scene.

"What the hell makes you think I want to get married, you asshole? I told you a hundred times, I don't want any of this. It's my damn family making me do it."

Bay couldn't believe her ears. If he was talking like this now, what would happen after the ceremony? Bay wanted to warn the poor bride. She seemed like a nice woman, and Bay could see that she didn't deserve to have a bad man like her cousin as her husband. Just then, unfortunately, Bay's mother emerged from the café, grabbed her by the arm, and dragged her inside.

"Where have you been? Grandpa and Grandma want to talk to you."

Inside the coffee house, Bay turned and surreptitiously scowled at her mother as she yanked her arm free and made a slight bow to her grandparents.

"Ah-Gong *hao*. Ah-Ma *hao*."

The old people touched her hands and her hair, and complimented her new dress. Bay was about to take off again when her father put his hands on her shoulders. "We're leaving. We should say congratulations and good luck to the lucky couple. Where are they?"

"The bride is in the church blowing up balloons," Bay said.

"Balloons?" Bay's mother frowned.

"I think we should help her," Bay said eagerly.

"We really have to go—no time to play with balloons. We'll drop Ah-Gong and Ah-Ma off at Uncle Chun's place and go home," Bay's father said.

Leaning her chin on the back of the seat, Bay watched the church shrink as the family car pulled down the street.

The seatbelt for the middle seat was broken, and in its absence, she didn't feel obligated to sit in any particular way.

"Sit down properly or you'll get carsick, Bay," her mother scolded. "And close your legs and put your hands on your knees, you're wearing a dress."

Bay did as she was told, but after a few minutes of silence, she could no longer hold back.

"I think they shouldn't get married," she blurted out.

"Why not?" her grandfather asked, tilting his head in her direction.

"He said he didn't want to marry her on the phone. I heard him. And he made her blow up balloons all by herself."

"Silly child. What do balloons have to do with anything?" Her grandmother dismissed her concern with a wave of her hand.

"Don't tell the bride what you heard, or the wedding might be called off." Bay's grandfather chuckled, but he pulled his lips into a straight line when he sensed his wife's burning glare.

"You keep your mouth shut. Don't go spreading rumors. Sometimes people say things they don't mean." The fierceness in her grandmother's voice made Bay lower her head, and the scolding continued. "Children should keep their mouths shut about the affairs of adults. Besides, we have all spent a great deal of money on that wedding. Marriage is no child's play. There are a great many responsibilities in life."

Bay slumped over, buried her face in the ruffles of her skirt, and sulked all the way home.

Round tables draped in red and chairs tied with giant pink bows filled a ballroom decorated in every corner with the red letter *si*, double spring, the wedding blessing. As luck would have it, a couple had broken off their engagement last second and made it possible for Bay's cousin to have a banquet at the lavish Gwan Hwa Hotel, in banquet room number two. Platters of food arrived at the tables, where the adults grew talkative and loud. Guests gossiped while they picked up strands of pickled sea cucumbers, seaweed, cured beef, and drunk chicken with heavy plastic chopsticks.

Bay rolled her eyes as the grown-ups at her table inappropriately teased her about when she was going to get married. Look at her cousins—one married, the other obediently going on blind dates arranged by her parents. Everyone seemed to forget that she was only eleven years old and that they had just made her wear a flower girl's wreath in her hair. She sipped two glasses of Little Red Berry, a nonalcoholic cranberry cocktail, one after the other, in silence, while trying to tune out the noise.

"Where is the bathroom?" Bay asked no one in particular.

"Over there, dearie." An aunt pointed toward large red doors at the other end of the banquet room.

"Do you want me to go with you?" Bay's mother asked.

"I may not be old enough to marry, but I'm old enough to use the bathroom myself, thanks."

The other adults at the table laughed awkwardly while Bay's mother shook her head apologetically, embarrassed by her daughter's brashness.

After slipping through the red doors, the signage on the wall presented Bay with two options—turn left to the bathroom, or right to the "bridal preparation room." She thought about this for a second and turned right.

Inside the preparation room, the bride sat alone before a long mirror illuminated by vanity lights, wearing a traditional Chinese *qipao* of red and gold. She dabbed her face with a powder puff, though it didn't look like her caked-over skin could hold any more makeup. She started when she finally noticed Bay. She blinked her long, heavy lashes in an uncomfortable way that showed she had never worn fake lashes before in her life.

"You look nice without glasses," Bay said.

The bride's bright red lips formed a smile. "You're the flower girl, aren't you? Thank you for helping. How old are you?"

"Eleven."

"Eleven years old," the bride repeated, drawing out the words, *shi yi sui*, as if in a trance. Maybe she was recalling when she herself was eleven.

"Actually, I have something to tell you," Bay said.

"Yes?" The bride turned to face her, something most adults didn't bother to do. Bay wished she hadn't, however, because of what she was about to say.

"I heard . . . your husband talking on the phone yesterday. He said that he didn't want to marry you."

"Pardon me?"

"I'm sorry, my family said I shouldn't tell you, but now you're already married so there's no wedding ceremony to ruin—"

"What exactly did he say?"

The bride's eyes were turning red again, like when she was blowing the balloons, and her slender hands shifted to her abdomen.

"That our family made him do it, and he didn't really want to get married . . . " Bay's voice trailed off.

At that moment, Bay's grandmother entered the room. "What on earth are you doing here, you naughty child?"

"I . . . I was looking for the bathroom and got lost." Bay bit her lips.

"And what's the matter with you?" The old woman noticed a tear roll down the bride's cheek and somehow intuited what had happened. "Never mind what silly children say. Whatever she said, it's nonsense."

The bride dabbed her eye with a tissue and sat upright in the chair. "On the contrary," she said, "children hear everything. They tell the truth."

Bay loved the bride even more now—a kindergarten teacher with a heart of gold. The bride had defended children all over the world against mean Grandma, even as her own heart was breaking.

Twenty minutes later, as if the scene in the bride's room had never happened, the bride and groom were toasting relatives and friends at every table, as was the custom. When the new couple came to her table, the bride smiled at Bay. "*Mei gwan si*, it's okay," she mouthed to her.

Three years later, Bay was spending most of her waking hours in classes at school or study sessions in the library and after school, she continued studying and completing practice exam books that her grandmother bought her.

"If you get good grades, then you can have a good career, maybe a steady government job in the future. If you have no education, all you can do is become a kindergarten teacher."

"What's wrong with kindergarten teachers?" Bay clicked her automatic pencil too many times and stabbed it into her exam book hard, snapping the lead.

"You remember your cousin-in-law? The one with the big stomach?"

Bay nodded, waiting.

"She and your cousin fought every day after the wedding, and the two of them went and got a divorce by themselves, without even consulting us."

"What about the baby?"

"It's a huge mess. The kid gets shipped back and forth between schools in different towns, between his mom, dad, and two sets of grandparents."

Bay felt a knot in her stomach. She thought of her cousin swearing behind the daffodils, and the lovely kindergarten teacher blowing pink-and-white balloons in the cold church. She even tried to imagine what their baby looked like. Grandmother was wrong; Bay had learned something from her cousin's marriage. And it wasn't what the adults would have thought.

Fifteen

Ellie was only fifteen when she lost her virginity to a boy on the empty stage of the auditorium in the music building of Taipei Preparatory Music School.

Ellie's piano skills were above average at best, but Kai—now, Kai was a star violinist, the concertmaster, the golden boy who stood before the entire orchestra with his two-hundred-year-old Stradivarius. At the beginning of each orchestra practice, he'd make a gesture toward the pianist to pound out a crisp, resounding middle A, tune his violin accordingly, and lead the strings, woodwinds, and brass instruments in turn with his mellow, rich delivery of the A, as they turned knobs, pressed buttons, and adjusted mouth pieces. Whenever the student orchestra performed a symphony with a violin solo, Kai stood center stage, awing the audience with technique-driven cadenzas he was known for composing himself in his five-lined notebook.

Kai could have asked anybody to be his piano accompaniment for the upcoming end-of-the-year concert, but he asked Ellie. Hands in his pockets, head tilted casually, no big deal, just asked her in passing if she was interested. *Sure,* she said, all nonchalant, playing it cool, though inside she was screaming, *yes oh yes oh my god YES*, and she wanted to scream *YAASS!* from the well-lit stage of a packed auditorium.

They practiced during lunchtime almost every day at school, the tension between them palpable in a way both titillating and painful to Ellie.

One weekend she finally found the courage to invite Kai over to her parents' apartment to listen to a rare recording. She had saved up her allowance to buy an imported platinum-edition CD from the classical music section of Tower Records. It included a live recording of the music they would be performing, a postmodern piece called *Untitled XX IV* by Zuzitte. In her bedroom, Kai kneeled in front of her little CD player, which vibrated with the sliding, abstract violin notes sprinkled amidst soft piano chords. His body seemed to hum and dance to the music, and Ellie thought her heart would burst from sheer longing, though she wasn't exactly sure specifically what for. After he left, she knelt in the same spot that Kai had kneeled an hour ago and slowly lowered her face to the floor, imagining what it would be like to be close to him.

A few days later, Kai surprised her with an invitation. "Let's sneak onto the stage and practice after school. The music hall will be dark since the control room's locked, but we can play from memory. It will be good practice."

Lies were concocted for their parents, something about a group project meeting in a fast-food restaurant. In reality, after leaving the school gate at 5:30 p.m. with their classmates, Kai, with his violin case slung across his torso, and Ellie, wearing her pounding heart on her sleeve, walked halfway around the school fence and reentered from the back gate. The music building wasn't locked yet, and they dashed in through the unsupervised front door and up the stairs to the concert hall.

The only lights barely illuminating the concert hall were the green EXIT lights above the four doors at the four corners of the room, watching them like narrowed eyes. The audience area was a sea of burgundy velour-covered chairs. One of the seats, hinge loosened, hung down like a sagging tongue. The piano on the stage glimmered faintly, reflecting the eerie green of the EXIT lights.

"Let's go onstage." Kai took Ellie's hand.

Her heart beat fast. The touch of his warm, string-calloused fingers made her tingle. She let Kai lead her to the middle of the stage, where he gestured for her to face the audience, so they could pretend to take a bow together, still holding hands. In that moment Ellie felt the rush of performing with violin prodigy Kai in front of the whole school; she pictured the applauding audience yelling *Encore!* loudly as they rose from their seats, all the girls' faces filled with envy.

Something interrupted her fantasy. Kai's hands were on her shoulders at first, but slowly they slid down to her chest, which was still quite flat. Self-conscious, she hunched her upper body slightly. His fingers lingered on her breasts briefly before shifting to her waist. Her heartbeat was deafening as she felt his hands through the pleated folds of her rough uniform skirt. Then, Kai's fingers reached under the skirt and found her panties, nudging them down. How did he know what to do? Had he done this before? Was this why he had asked her to play the piano accompaniment for him?

Ellie was so stunned that she stood, statue-like, allowing Kai to kneel before her as he had before the CD player. He kissed her "down there," her first kiss from him landing in a spot she had never imagined it would land. Then he stood up to kiss her on the lips. The taste caught Ellie by surprise, but it did not repulse her. Kai took her hands and put them around his waist.

"Undo my belt," he said.

Ellie did as she was told, and down came his uniform pants. Through the green fabric of his fitted underpants, Ellie could see the shape of what looked like the stalk of a shitake mushroom.

The mushroom did not stay firm for long. Soon it turned bright red and slimy and was hidden away again. It all happened so quickly and quietly in the dark that Ellie felt like she had only dreamt it.

They both acted as they normally did the next day at school and practiced like usual during the lunch hour. Secretly, however, Ellie felt like she was floating in cottony clouds, on a warm river, in thin air. She was in love. Kai winked at her in math class and she spent the rest of the hour doodling his name along with musical notes and hearts in her textbook.

Weeks later, with some horror as the euphoria subsided, she wondered why she had not needed a sanitary napkin for so long. But it was just once—what were the odds? Was Kai such a genius and prodigy he could impregnate on the first try too?

Ellie tried two different pregnancy tests: one inconclusive and one positive, the tiny plus sign like the cross she felt she would be crucified on once her family found out. This was exactly the kind of luck she had in life—drawing the short bamboo stick from the teacher's cup to clean the girls' bathrooms, never winning anything in a raffle, called first for physical exams in PE, and now, having barely had sex once, fumbling and passive in the dark, and bam, knocked up! She wished she could undo the conception, without undoing what she and Kai had shared. She knew she didn't want a baby. At fifteen, she had barely grown out of stuffed animals and dolls. Totoros and Tarepandas still lined her bed. She had a Sailor Moon anime poster featuring a magical wand-wielding girl with yellow pigtails in a schoolgirl uniform on her wall. Hers was not the room of a mother.

Ellie decided not to deal with it for as long as possible. There was a wisdom to the method of ostriches—once upon a time she thought they were the stupidest creatures, evolutionarily unfit, etc.—she now understood. Sometimes, life was just too much. It was better to hide and pretend.

She missed one period, two periods, three periods. Her stomach barely swelled against her thin frame, her morning sickness was minimal, and nobody suspected anything or asked any questions. She wondered about telling her parents, telling Kai, telling somebody—anybody who could help. She was too scared to have an abortion because she'd heard all the stories about the blood-soaked ghost fetuses that followed around women who'd had them. She didn't want to be haunted by a sad baby spirit for the rest of her life. Ellie was terrified of ghosts, more terrified than she was of labor or of her father beating her to death when he found out the truth. She was not even supposed to hold hands with a boy, let alone have a boyfriend or become impregnated by him. Unthinkable.

The night of the end-of-semester concert, Kai performed beautifully on the violin. Ellie did not hit one wrong note on the piano. Kai reached for Ellie's hand when they bowed together, and they held hands tightly for a few seconds. The audience's applause was deafening, the stage lights blinding. In that moment, Ellie thought everything would be alright: she and Kai would become a young married couple, the baby would be incredibly independent and easy to take care of, possibly a musical prodigy like its father. They would all live happily ever after.

But her belly was beginning to show. It did not take long for her mother to corner her and extract a confession. The school sent a letter ordering that Ellie be transferred to another institution. The board of the exclusive music school did not want a pregnant teen in their classrooms, nor did they want her walking around in Taipei with her belly bulging beneath the school logo on her uniform, sullying their reputation. At home, Ellie's mother covered for her for as long as she could, but when Ellie's father found out, he came after Ellie with a cleaver.

Following the advice of a family friend, Ellie's mother transferred Ellie to a boarding school for girls in rural southern Taiwan, partly for her safety. At her new country school, all the girls stared. Most of them had never had a boyfriend in their lives, and they called Ellie names: Slut, Trash, Worn Shoe.

The baby girl died within a month of being born, ten weeks premature, weak and unable to breathe on her own. Ellie never held her and turned away when the infant was offered to her, covered in tubes and tape, attached to beeping monitors. She tried to forget its face: a pink, raw blur with closed slits for eyes. It did not look like her and did not look like Kai, whom she never saw again.

Yuan Zu Socializing

YOU KNOW WHAT *yuan zu* socializing is, right? Like in Japan, when the high school girls date older, usually married men in exchange for money—that kind of socializing. *Yuan zu*, to "help" the girls' pockets. You know how expensive clothes and cute knick-knacks are in Japan. Don't be too fast to judge them. This happens in Taiwan, too. I should know, because I am one of those girls.

I attend First Girls' Senior High night division—this fact is very good for business. I saunter down the sidewalk in First Girls' olive-colored shirt and black pleated skirt, and everyone in the streets turn their heads. Not that the uniform is attractive—it's ugly as road kill—but it's a status symbol. Only the smartest of the smart and most studious girls get into my senior high; that's why it's called "First Girls'." So if a girl wearing a dirty green shirt climbs onto a bus, or walks into a 7-11, you stare. You wonder, how did she get so smart? You think, she will become a diplomat or president or CEO or doctor one day, no doubt.

Look carefully, though. First Girls' is divided into day and night school. The geniuses go to the day school. Their

IDs are stitched in a rich, yellow thread. Girls like me, who couldn't get into any other senior high anywhere, public or private, pay a lot to go to the night school, which is the exact opposite of the day school. Day girls have their hair cut below the ear; they study all day and all night. Their uniforms are neatly ironed, creased, and their skirts fall slightly below the knee. A lot of night girls work during the day, or lounge in bed with their live-in boyfriends. Night girls are identifiable by the white rather than yellow thread that the uniform lady uses to stitch our IDs, and our skirts are also unique. They are either very short, almost mid-thigh for those of us who have nice legs, or especially long, to cover platform black leather shoes, which day girls would never be allowed to wear to school.

My skirt is short, way short. I wake up around noon every day, wiggle into my uniform mini, put on white elephant-style socks which I bunch down to flatter the shape of my calves, and slip into my shiny platforms. When I leave the house, my mother is still at the morning market, buying food, gossiping, browsing racks of cheap clothing. She's kind of a clone—she's like any other *obasan*, a middle-aged lady who speaks loudly with a coarse Taiwanese accent, has eyebrows tinted a strange shade of bluish-blackish purple, steadily puts on ten pounds every decade, and complains all day about her husband and daughter.

Skipping breakfast, I head toward McDonald's with my schoolbag, which is almost completely empty. I leave all my textbooks at school. I never study anyway, and carrying heavy books would stunt my growth and ruin the shape of my legs. I will allow nothing to ruin these legs, my nicest feature. So what if my eyes are small and slanted and single-lidded, my nose flat and upturned, my lips thin and too wide. My mom was no belle, so my not looking like Miss Taiwan is no surprise. But that's okay. I have a Miss Taiwan figure. I pencil in my eyebrows carefully with a light-brown pencil, my hair is dyed brownish-yellow with feathered edges that flutter in the wind—I look better than one of those four-eyed, snooty day-school girls any day.

I browse merchandise in cute little stores, eat at road-side stands, and either listen to records in the record store or sit in McDonald's until 5:30 p.m. every day. Sometimes I even meet a middle-aged man for a quickie during his lunch or afternoon break. Occasionally, all they want is some conversation or my underwear for a keepsake—poor, gutless, emasculated men. Some of them want more, and pay more, and we go to hotels and motels to "rest," the euphemistic term for renting a bed and privacy for two hours to screw. It never takes two hours, needless to say. Thirty minutes would be long, including the undressing, dressing, and showers. I charge one thousand NT an hour. All men look the same naked. With their respectable-looking suits on, these men are not that different from my dad. In fact, naked or clothed, they are my dad; they are exactly the same.

Ever since I remember, my mother always yelled at my father, who never came home at a decent hour. As I grew up, I learned that my dad, my hero, my role model who, once upon a time, took me to amusement parks, propped me on his shoulders in the night market, and brought home gifts after business trips—he had little girlfriends. He went out with teenage girls, took them out to eat, bought them presents, and kept their dirty undergarments in a different secret drawer every time, which my mother would eventually discover and throw out in a fit, wailing and invoking ancestors.

As soon as I was old enough to receive my first proposition, I had my revenge on the middle-aged men who were like my dad, who embarrassed their wives by doting on and sleeping with teenage girls, and who thought they could get away with abandoning their families and corrupting the innocent. I bought FM2 pills from a dealer recommended by one of my classmates who was also in the business. I look for him in a corner booth in McDonald's every Tuesday if I need more.

My first customer was also my first victim. I still remember how he looked as he approached me, greasy hair balding at the dividing point in the center of his scalp, his beady rat's eyes, ill-fitting gray suit, and crocodile briefcase. I smiled and flipped my braids at him and he asked me in a low voice if I would like to go to a motel. I asked him for some refreshments from 7-11 first, which he promptly bought. Then, once in the hotel room, I told him to take a shower (no favors otherwise) while I slipped the powdery contents of a capsule into his drink, an energy soda. The pathetic man needed some ginseng in soda pop to make him feel more virile. I didn't even have to remove my clothes that time—the pill did its job and my first naked businessman passed out quickly. I didn't kick my first customer, though later on I developed the habit of adding a dusty footprint to their white shirts, writing on their faces with my Dior lipstick, or spraying them all over with strong, cheap perfume, so their wives would give them hell later. Naturally, I emptied the contents of that man's and every other man's wallet into my purse—a little something for me to remember them by.

These men can't go to the police about me because their crime is greater than mine. Society would never condemn a young teenage girl instead of a dirty, middle-aged *sa zu*, sandy pig. The man is always the filthy one, the corrupter, the one who breaks promises, ruins relationships, messes up his own life and the lives of those around him. I believe I carry out a form of justice. What I occasionally do with customers; the unwashed underwear I sell; old men's freckled arms I hang on to; wrinkled, fallen bodies that I witness—these are a small sacrifice for the cause of punishing such men.

This afternoon, a man with a scar on his face looks at me a certain way on the street. So much comes unspoken. Swinging my hips so that the pleats of my uniform skirt dance, I stop at the corner so he can catch up with me. Sure enough, he approaches.

"Are you free tonight?" he asks in a low voice, but in a casual tone, like we're old friends, so no passersby will take notice.

"It depends. What do you have in mind?" I'm not sure about this man. He might be an undercover cop—certainly not the businessman type.

"I need a pretty one to go to the karaoke bar with me tonight; it's my friend's birthday. I don't want a dirty karaoke princess, they're full of diseases. You look like a nice, clean girl. Smart, too, First Girls' Senior High."

I feel flattered that he pretends there is no difference between day school and night school. And that he thinks I'm different from the karaoke joint whores. When he lifts his hand to brush his hair away from the scar on his forehead, I see what his sleeve had concealed—the bottom of a green, purple, blue, and red dragon tattoo that goes all around his arm. This is no policeman.

"1000 NT an hour, just karaoke," I say.

"Just karaoke." He nods. "Eleven o'clock, Big Loud Chef Karaoke Restaurant, suite two, under the name Mr. Chen."

He reaches into his pants and loosens five one-thousand-NT bills from a bundle.

"Five thousand, that's at least four hours, and I'll call a taxi to send you home if you get tired early. Here's two thousand now, and I'll give you the rest tonight."

I smile, accepting the cash.

In ten minutes, I am calling my mother to tell her that I will be staying over at my friend Ah Mei's house tonight because her parents are out of town and she wants company. This excuse Mom has heard a hundred times and presumably believes. She grunts, saying that she puts on weight because nobody comes home to eat and she ends up putting everything she cooked in her own stomach.

"Sorry, Ma," I say, "but Ah Mei needs me."

"Go, go," she replies. "Just as well. Don't watch soap operas all night. The two of you should do your homework."

"We sure will, Ma, don't you worry."

I'm not entirely lying. Ah Mei's parents are out of town in a larger sense: they are dead. She and her brother live alone in a junky apartment near Taiping Temple. I go there whenever I have a late night. I call Ah Mei next, inviting her to come out and help spend my cash. Ah Mei doesn't go to school or anything; I think she just watches cable TV all day. Her brother works in an insurance office, and their aunts and uncles give them enough red envelope money on birthdays and every possible holiday to help them get by.

By the time I have almost finished my golden Filet-O-Fish, Ah Mei sits down across from me in a yellow McDonald's seat and helps herself to my fries.

"Let's go to the cosmetics counter at SOGO, get our makeup done by the ladies, and buy everything they use on our faces," Ah Mei says.

She has no makeup on her face, and some marks on her cheek tell me that she was sleeping on a wrinkled pillowcase no more than twenty minutes ago.

"Sure," I say.

Cosmetics counter ladies are usually mean, but not to young, reckless spenders like us. We have smooth, unblemished skin, but often buy more lotions, perfumes, and powders than wealthy housewives with facelifts and multiple plastic surgeries.

Soon the cash is gone and I move on to swiping my credit card. Ah Mei and I, faces freshly painted and holding little pastel green and pink bags which hold our purchases and free gifts, top off the shopping spree with a nice Japanese dinner on the top floor of the department store. Spicy seafood noodles and green tea with red bean ice cream for me, fried vegetable *ten don* and sweet yam ice cream for Ah Mei. Much better than my mom's cooking. My mom thinks the shelf life for leftovers is infinite, and always buys the cheapest fish with hardly any meat and a hundred thousand little bones in them. Getting one of those damn thorns stuck in your throat is enough to put you off fish forever. I can kind of understand why Dad would rather eat outside.

Satiated by our meal, we get a taxi which drops me off at the gate of First Girls' and then takes Ah Mei back to her apartment.

I am forty-five minutes late for class, but nobody cares. The biology teacher doesn't even look at me when I walk in. He is completely absorbed in the act of drawing some kind of molecular structure on the blackboard. I used to like biology, but then I came to a realization: what's the point? (There is none.) My classmates must have had similar epiphanies. They are combing or braiding their hair, touching up their makeup in small mirrors, sleeping on bent elbows, or scribbling words on scented stationery. Tan Ni, sitting to the right of me, passes me a note: *Nice makeup. Did it yourself?*

No, I write back. *Cosmetics counter at SOGO.*

Big spender, she scribbles back.

I'm not sure how to take this comment, so I crumple the note and take a comic book out from inside my desk to read instead of replying.

Later that night, at Big Loud Chef Karaoke, I arrive fashionably late, still in my green and black uniform. The man who has hired me, who tells me to call him Ren Second Brother, introduces me as his favorite *mei mei*, little sister. Three karaoke princesses in revealing clothes and high heels are already sitting with five other men between the ages of twenty-five and thirty-five. So much for not hiring princesses. Blue velvet sofas line the room, and a giant TV screen is playing a sexy music video with dancing women in bikinis.

Ren makes room for me next to him and hands me a drink. "Just came in with the waiter, I promise it's good."

The princesses are already sipping similar cocktails, and they nod at me. I'd been thirsty all day, especially after the salty restaurant food. My drink looks tropical, bright red with a slice of orange on the glass, and I like the way it tastes on my tongue: sweet, tangy, with a trace of bitter alcohol. In no time I am enjoying myself with these total strangers, even though the karaoke working girls can't sing and keep nagging the men to purchase a few more hours of their time and order more oysters and shrimp at exorbitant prices to go with the drinks. People fight for the microphone, clap when someone sings well, and laugh when someone is too drunk to get the lyrics right. The karaoke princesses can never agree on what song to pick next. For women who do this for a living, they sure can't carry a tune worth a damn.

At one point I feel tired and dizzy, and lean back against Ren on the sofa. He puts his arm around me and guides me to fall into his lap, which is warm, hard and soft at the same time. The next thing I know I seem to be dreaming, my surroundings fading around me, strange, why am I sleepy so early, I am relaxed, so relaxed, floating above my body, feeling safe and content.

After what seems like a full night's sleep, I wake up, groggy and disoriented, to the coarse Taiwanese accent of a cleaning lady. "*Wei*, time to get up. Here are your clothes."

She is covering me with my green uniform shirt. She reminds me of my mom.

I realize that I am completely naked. I feel soreness down there, and when my right hand brushes against my crotch, I find an unmistakable, slippery, sticky substance, a lot of it, still leaking from my body. Some of it close to the edges has crusted. The cleaning woman now has her back to me, and is wiping the table. I put on my white panties quietly, then my skirt. I hook my designer bra in the back and button my green First Girls' shirt. How many men? How many times? What of my revenge?

Lock, Stock, and Two Smoking Barrels

SONNIE MU DID not know that he was looking for love when he entered an internet chat room called "Gay Chat."

He hardly believed there was such a thing as love, at least for him.

He had never wanted the pretty girls that every boy had a crush on as he grew up. Instead, he gazed secretly at his male coevals, admiring their athletic prowess on the basketball field, their taut muscles, their dark, lively eyes. His own eyes were soft and, remarkably, his left eye was dark gray while his right eye was brown. His friends called him yin-yang eyes; he was supposed to be able to see ghosts. Sonnie never saw ghosts. All he saw were boys, boys he couldn't have and shouldn't approach, boys who soon had girls hanging off their arms, and boys who slapped him hard on the back and whose friendly gestures he was too shy to return.

Sonnie did not grow up with many boys, anyway. He was always in music school, which meant that in a class of twenty-six boys and girls, there were usually two to four boys, one of whom was Sonnie, and the rest of his classmates were piano-playing, perfumed, spoiled, rich girls. They were pretty, proper, talented, and usually nice, but they were not for him.

Now, as a bachelor of thirty-two, Sonnie liked his self-sufficient life in Taipei. His parents had him in their old age, so he had very few memories of them except their somber, quiet presence at the dinner table and their handing him red envelopes during Chinese New Year. He loved them, vaguely and mostly out of politeness. When they died of cancer when he was eight, he cried only in his sleep. Perhaps he was too young to understand death then. His older brother, a man of few words, and sister, a very traditional woman, were the ones who brought him up. But like estranged parents, each of them had long since moved to different parts of Taiwan. His brother lived in Yi Lan because of his job with the government-owned telecom company, and his sister went even further south to Kaohsiung after marrying a schoolteacher there.

This left Sonnie with their old family house, a modest three-bedroom, one-story house which belonged to one of the historic neighborhoods in Taipei close to the old train station. Most of the traditional houses with large gardens and little sheds nearby had been torn up and rebuilt into skyscrapers, but not Sonnie's neighborhood. The owners here were all too stubborn or old-fashioned to sell their property and move. Sonnie liked his neighborhood; here he felt safe. It was like holding on to some part of his child-hood, before he knew that he was different, before he had to worry about boys, or men, or what people thought of him. This was where he had practiced his violin one and a half hours a day, seven days a week, for twenty-five years, and this was where his violin students came for private lessons before big recitals, important exams, and to fill the hours of the day during winter and summer vacation.

Sonnie taught violin at two music schools, making slightly less than a typical elementary school teacher. The private lessons he gave to students outside of school and other private students, however, more than made up for his modest taxable income. He always had thousand-NT dollar bills lying around in clean, white envelopes with "Teacher Mu" written on them. These he spent on nice suits for eve-nings at the concert hall. His drawers contained imported Calvin Klein underwear and silk-blend socks, handcrafted leather belts and silk neckties. He lived comfortably but not extravagantly, taking pleasure in little things like fine gar-ments and nice, solitary meals at a good restaurant.

He was the quintessential Taiwanese bachelor, the es-tablished thirty-something young man with a house and car and job whom every mother wanted her daughter to marry. Many people were interested in arranging for him to go on blind dates with their daughters or sisters or friends, but he always declined by saying he did not feel ready for such a commitment yet. In truth, he would not be able to commit to a woman until his next lifetime. In Asia, unfortunately, one did not turn around and ask the parents trying to offer one their daughter whether they had a nice son for one to date. It simply wasn't done. The word "gay" did not really exist unless you were making fun of someone, calling them *bo li*, glass, a name Sonnie never understood. Why were gay people referred to as "glass"? Because they were invisible, and one looked right past them? It was certainly how Sonnie felt. He was under the impression that even if he ran down the street, screaming at the top of his lungs, "I like men, not women!" the old lady next door would continue to push her eligible grand-niece on him and tell him that he was just "going through a phase."

One evening, Sonnie stumbled into the gay chat room on a Taiwanese website, Yam.com, and found himself typing in English to a man called Brian.

"Where are you from?" Sonnie typed.

"Great Britain," Brian answered.

Sonnie's heart skipped a little; he had never had a conversation with a white man before. He had seen them at fancy concerts with their Taiwanese wives, in posh outdoor bars drinking beer. He never thought that he could get a gay white man to talk to him. But Westerners were supposed to be more liberated and open-minded, and maybe this was exactly what he needed.

"You live in Taipei?" Sonnie asked.

"Yes, I work here."

"You like it here? Taipei?"

"Not really."

The conversation was slow, but Brian sent Sonnie a picture of himself and asked if he would like to go out and have a drink of tea or coffee sometime. Fumbling to find the computer keys to type his answer, Sonnie felt his body humming with nervous excitement as he made his first blind date: a date with a white man, a British person, someone with an elegant accent, light skin, and from the looks of the photograph, a fit, muscular body. Sonnie felt like his life was about to change, like he was finally breaking free of some kind of shell.

They were supposed to meet on the first floor of the plaza beside the old train station at seven in the evening. Sonnie left home early to have a tasty meal of crab bisque in a toasted sourdough bread bowl on the top floor of a nearby department store. Afterward, he stood reading a novel in a bookstore beside the restaurant, as he'd had the habit of reading entire books in bookstores since he was a child.

Sonnie did not know if he had read his watch wrong earlier or simply lost himself in the book by a Nobel Prize–winning Chinese author (it wasn't interesting at all, in fact), but all of a sudden he saw that the hands of the large clock in the bookstore were pointing at eight and five. He was almost an hour late!

Taking the elevator and wishing it moved more quickly down the twenty-one stories, he half ran toward the plaza, thinking that he had missed Brian, who would have assumed that he had been stood up and left. Who makes a date with someone in an online chat room, anyway? As his eyes scanned the plaza full of commuting office workers, and schoolgirls and schoolboys going to cram schools or shopping, Sonnie spotted a Caucasian man of medium build wearing ripped jeans and a dingy wife beater. Sonnie himself wore casual khaki trousers, a carefully pressed shirt and a handcrafted, Indian-style leather belt. As Sonnie approached, the two men looked at each other and shared what seemed like a moment of recognition.

"You are Brian?" Sonnie ventured.

A nod. "You Sonnie from the chat room?" Brian pronounced his name *sunny*, which sounded odd, but Sonnie nodded. For all he knew, he had been pronouncing his own English name wrong this whole time.

It was a good thing Sonnie didn't really sweat; he was overheated from running and very embarrassed for being almost an hour late. If one were half an hour late for an exam the teacher wouldn't even let one in—Sonnie felt grateful that this gruff-looking yet in some ways beautiful foreigner had stood there waiting for him for a full fifty-three minutes (assuming the man had arrived on time).

"I'm so sorry I am late, I made a mistake," Sonnie said, then realized that he was not making a good first impression, what with his accent, nervousness, and lack of confidence.

He collected himself and nodded in the direction of some stores. "What you want to do? Drink alcohol?"

Then Sonnie thought that this was probably the wrong thing to say, too—to assume that all British people wanted to drink.

"I don't like the drinks they serve here," Brian replied. "And they're totally overpriced, even though they've only got bottled stuff here. I'll tell you what, let's go to an MTV, I know one nearby." He pronounced bottled *bah-old*, which threw Sonnie for a second, but he nodded and followed Brian's lead.

Sonnie had never been to an MTV in his life. To him, those were dirty places where strange things took place. Usually lovers went there, rented a room and a movie and watched it there in comfortable privacy (not complete privacy, though—likely for legal reasons, there was a small glass window about the size of a fist in the door). Teenage delinquents went there, and drug addicts, too, when they could afford it.

Sonnie patted his pants as if subconsciously brushing them clean as he and Brian walked into a dark neighborhood, where blood-like betel nut juice stained the asphalt and the streets themselves smelled. They passed stray dogs, garbage stacked beside the road, tobacco shops, places that sold lottery tickets, and an amputated man crawling along the sidewalk, pushing a tray with him, begging for money. Sonnie considered putting some change in the handicapped beggar's tray, then remembered stories about how some beggars pretend to be helpless, but if you get too close to them, their accomplices, a group of muggers, will jump you. He quickened his step to catch up with Brian.

The MTV was a tiny business hidden on the sixth floor of a sleazy-looking cement building with tinted windows. Brian knew his way around. Soon the two men were at the service counter in the MTV, being invited to pick a film to watch.

Before the catalogue had been presented to them, Sonnie clumsily dug out his wallet.

"Please, let me pay. I am so sorry I was late. I feel bad. Do you mind?"

"Sure," Brian said, hands in pockets, indifferent. "What do you want to watch, bruv?"

"You can pick."

"Okay." Brian flipped through pages until he landed one finger on a page. "Let's watch this one, *Lock, Stock, and Two Smoking Barrels*. It will be an educational experience for you, since it's about Great Britain, my motherland."

Without catching a word of the movie's long title, Sonnie nodded eagerly and gave the clerk a five hundred-NT bill and two one-hundred-NT bills. A middle-aged woman with deep, tired marks and bags under her eyes led the two men to a large room. She opened the door and turned on the lights so they could have a look inside.

"Okay?" she asked, referring to the room.

"Fine," Brian said.

"Yes, yes, good," Sonnie said, speaking in English.

The woman cast a strange look at him, as if judging him for being with a man or for being with a foreigner, possibly both, but walked away too quickly for Sonnie to tell.

Lock, Stock, and Two Smoking Barrels turned out long, violent, strange, and mostly incomprehensible for Sonnie. He found himself unable to settle down comfortably in the room alone with this foreign man and foreign film despite an abundance of pillows and sofa space. Half the room was sofa. It stretched out long and wide, like a bed with armrests on the sides. Brian, who laughed out loud in an almost sinister way, especially when someone got shot, periodically turned to Sonnie and asked if he "got" what happened.

"You know what it meant when the big guy said *crystal*?"

"Uh . . . crystal clear?"

Sonnie had read as much as he could in English, listened to the English-language ICRT radio station, and kept current with his vocabulary by reading *Studio Classroom* magazine, but this was a difficult question for him.

"Right. Good job." Brian looked pleased and turned his closely shaven head back to the large screen. He was leaning alternatively on his right and left elbows, flopping belly down on the sofa.

"Make yourself more comfortable. Are you comfortable like that?" he asked Sonnie, who was visibly stiff and tensed up whenever characters cursed or fired a gun.

Sonnie nodded, though just that moment he started at a loud gunshot.

"You can move closer to me if you like," Brian said.

"It's okay, I am fine here." Sonnie's heart brimmed with hope, but he was too shy to accept. Maybe if Brian had insisted, or asked a second time, he would reconsider, but he didn't.

Sonnie longed to stretch his cramped legs. He imagined the handsome foreigner putting his arm around his shoulders—was that what was supposed to happen? He had so little experience, and the porn he occasionally furtively looked at on the internet was low quality and fuzzy. It didn't show much gray area between two people meeting for the first time and the same two people going at it vigorously moments later. Plus, the situations were foreign and outlandish, involving pizza deliveries or flight school, or even the great outdoors, complete with waterfalls, boulders, and forests.

Sonnie made a mental note to himself to watch more British movies in the future so he could understand the accent better, especially if he and Brian went to an MTV in the future and watched something like this again. Understanding the film would help him feel more at ease.

"This is the kind of life I grew up with," Brian said at the end of the movie.

Sonnie blinked, thinking of the smoking guns and mobsters.

Brian continued. "We had to struggle, just my mum and me; we were very poor. Most Taiwanese I meet don't understand."

Sonnie, who wanted very much to understand, nodded as sympathetically as possible, but Brian simply sighed and got up.

Sonnie walked Brian to a bus stop where he could catch a bus to his apartment near National Taiwan Normal University, where a lot of foreigners and exchange students lived because of the Chinese classes offered by the university. Along the way, Brian only attempted conversation once, asking Sonnie about what he did for a living. Sonnie, struggling with his English, tried his best to talk about music school and spoiled rich kids, things he was familiar with. Brian did not respond enthusiastically, only making a few "I see" type remarks or clarifying English words that Sonnie had butchered beyond recognition.

The next evening, Sonnie was already in "Gay Chat" when Brian logged on. In fact, he had been waiting all day to talk to Brian again. He couldn't get him out of his mind.

"Hello!" Sonnie typed.

"Hi."

"Nice to talk to you again," Sonnie typed.

"I think we can't be friends."

"I think so, too," Sonnie replied immediately. He had accidentally read Brian's "can't" as "can."

"I said we cannot be friends." Brian typed, sensing that Sonnie had misunderstood.

Sonnie stopped for several seconds. It was like someone had dipped him into a bathtub of ice.

"Why?" he finally tapped onto his keyboard weakly.

"When you first saw me yesterday, your face fell. I could see it. I get the same response every time. When I go to an interview for a job teaching English, at a kindergarten, even—and I'm great with children—the same thing happens, and they don't hire me. They see that I am not wearing a nice shirt and tie and suit pants. They judge people by the cover, and that's wrong. A bit of hair on the chin, a pair of old jeans, and you're out. You judged me, too. When we met, you saw that I was not clean cut, and your face fell."

Sonnie was stunned. He read the terrible words slowly as they appeared on his computer screen. He had not been disappointed about Brian's appearance at all—he was too upset and embarrassed about being late. But Brian's words left him with a rotten feeling inside. He felt misunderstood, and somehow, dirty. He wanted to explain, in perfect British English, that he had not grown up particularly rich, that he was not who Brian thought he was, that he did not judge him for how he dressed or whether he had money, that he only wanted a chance to get to know him, that he was attracted to him. Sonnie wanted to tell Brian how much courage it took him to finally meet him in person, how hard it was to be gay in Taiwan, that he had thought about him practically every minute since their date at the MTV, how he longed for him to touch him, about how hopeful he had felt, how much he longed for a relationship, for a boyfriend.

"I did not think that way yesterday—" Sonnie began, but no words came. He could think of a hundred eloquent explanations in Chinese, but not in English.

"It's okay," Brian continued. "You and I come from very different backgrounds. I don't expect you to understand. I'm just saying that we can't be friends."

Defeated and hurt, Sonnie could only type, "Okay."

"Take care." The last words from Brian.

"Bye," Sonnie typed, after a long pause. He felt ashamed—an awful, festering shame, which, if manifested in his body, would show as beehive-like infections in all his soft tissue, his liver and heart all sponge-like, eaten away and shredded into three-dimensional, pink-and-blood-red lace filled with nothing but holes.

He shouldn't have entered the chat room, shouldn't have gone on a blind date with a stranger and foreigner; if he had done none of those things he would not have been hurt. Turning off his desktop computer, he leaned back in his seat and closed his eyes. He felt weak, like he had been eviscerated, scraped, and emptied out from the inside.

A Bach theme was coming to him, a melancholy one in G minor that always pained him with its stretched, split chords. He picked up his violin and played. He pulled the bow across the strings as if wiping away the memory of the past few hours, or rather, his entire lifetime. He would play and play beautifully until he felt better, or until a student came, a rich little spoiled kid with an expensive violin in a heavy, velvet-lined case, who had hardly any worries at all, at least for now.

And Then There Were None

Lily Gu stared into the vast blue nothingness beyond a little rectangular window with rounded edges. She rubbed a napkin against the grease mark left on the windowpane by her nose and thought moodily about her ex-girlfriend.

The flight from Victoria to Taipei took nearly twenty-four hours: two continental breakfasts, three three-course lunches, and a long layover in Japan. The whirring of the engines shifted as the descent began. Flight attendants rushed about locking up food carriers, making sure overhead bins were closed, and collecting empty champagne glasses. Lily pressed two buttons, one to lower the foot rest and straighten her chair, another to change the massage setting of her seat. She could afford flying business because her father's clinic in Taipei did well. He had also paid for her violin and voice lessons at the Victoria Conservatory of Music in Canada for the past five years.

Over ten years ago, local gangsters came to call at Mr. Gu's brand new clinic. Unless he paid them a monthly protection fee, they said, they would kidnap his daughter for ransom money. After an initial advance, Mr. Gu made other arrangements as soon as possible. He sent his wife and daughter to Canada. With the help of some relatives in Canada, he bought them an old, drafty house in Victoria. He visited them in Victoria or they visited him in Taipei twice a year.

Mrs. Gu, lonely in a foreign land and growing eccentric in her middle age, clung desperately to her daughter. She blamed Lily's interest in women on her husband's absence, reminding him every time he visited that it was because of him they would never have grandchildren.

"There are worse things than having a lesbian for a daughter," he said.

"Like what? Staying in Taiwan and being kidnapped by gangsters? Are those our only options?" Mrs. Gu spent a great deal of her free time thinking about what things would have been like had they stayed in Taipei. Often she spoke of the food she missed from the night market: the tasty dumplings, grilled squid, fried calamari, noodle soup.

"Besides, women can have babies however they want. Lily still might make grandparents out of us, if that's what she wants," Mr. Gu said.

"Easy for you to say. What do you happen to know about being a woman and raising a child all by yourself, without a father figure?"

For all of Mrs. Gu's complaining, she had little intention of returning to Taiwan, even when Lily told her she was moving to Taipei, at least temporarily, to teach music. Lily's Aunt Kitty, a music teacher, just married a man from Hong Kong, and had arranged for Lily to "inherit" her violin students in Taipei. The students didn't have to worry about finding a new teacher, and Lily got a job fresh out of the Conservatory, where she'd received barely passing grades, botched her final recital by going completely out-of-tune in one passage and forgetting the score in another. She knew they'd let her graduate out of pity because they thought she was an underachieving immigrant who didn't speak English. Just as well. She had been distracted, and her heart had never been in her music. Her life consisted of alternating conflicts: constant drama with her girlfriend and arguments at home.

"You are no daughter of mine," were Mrs. Gu's exact words the night she found out about Lily and Nina. She pushed Lily out into the snow and locked the door. Lily spent the night sobbing on Nina's futon. Days swelled into weeks, and with them some of the initial shock and pain faded. Lily and her mother learned to deal with each other, but just barely.

In the airport, the immigration officer waved Lily through the gate after a quick glance at her Taiwanese passport. The lines for "visitors" were long and slow-moving, but Lily had learned to use her Taiwanese passport when she visited and her Canadian one when she reentered Canada.

After claiming her luggage, Lily spotted her aunt in the crowd. Kitty, perfect skin, full figure, permed hair dyed reddish-brown, gushed over Lily and stroked Lily's mid-parted, long hair, the classic Asian-Canadian do.

"You're even taller than when I last saw you! You must be at least 168 centimeters, or more than 170? Just like a model! Models are very popular here in Taiwan now. But you are too thin. You should eat some more. What are they feeding you in Canada? Don't you think she's too thin, dear?" Kitty turned to her husband.

Instead of answering, Kitty's balding, bespectacled husband reached into his right pocket and produced a heavy, Bluebeard-worthy ring of keys. "You can wait over by the front entrance. I'll go get the car."

He shuffled away, keys jangling.

"Never mind him," Kitty said, watching her husband depart. "Low EQ, absolutely no social skills. But a nice man, really. Very generous. His family is from old Guomingtang money."

"I can't believe you're moving all the way to Hong Kong. What if you don't like it there?"

"What's not to like? Fantastic places to shop, good food, there's even horse racing and exclusive clubs. I've been there five times already and loved every moment of it."

Kitty stroked her classic Louis Vuitton shoulder bag and smiled. Lily wondered if it was fake, like every other Louis Vuitton bag carried in the streets of Taipei.

"Well, I hope you are happy with him," Lily said.

"I'm all set for life. Even if we get divorced, I'll get half his stuff. A real success story, huh?" Kitty seemed more pleased with herself than sarcastic.

Back at Lily's new one-bedroom apartment, which already had in it an old upright piano, Kitty took out a spiral-bound planner and opened it to a section filled with names and phone numbers.

"I have talked to these four kids, the ones whose names are highlighted, and they will be your new students. I told them you charge one thousand per hour, which isn't that much, but I thought it was appropriate since you're starting out. Is that alright?"

Lily nodded. She had no idea she was worth one thousand NT an hour, which was about 42 CAD, 35 USD.

"I already told them to call you to confirm their class schedules with you. This girl, Paoi Wu, is in junior high school. She's kind of slow and tone-deaf but she tries. These two are brother and sister. And this one, Guo Sun, is your age or maybe a year older. I told him not to fall in love with you, hee hee."

Thankfully, Kitty's cell phone rang so that Lily did not have to respond.

"Yes, I know the flight leaves at three! I'll be right down, hold your horses."

Kitty reached out to hug Lily, who reciprocated with a four-finger pat on her aunt's back, not knowing where to put her hands. Against her own slim torso, Kitty's body was like a lumpy down pillow. Lily wondered if she would ever find anyone like Nina here in Taipei. Kitty picked up her handbag and put on a pair of burgundy sunglasses which made her look like a gigantic fly.

"Don't have too much fun all by yourself in Taipei! Give me a call if you need help with something."

It took less than a week for Lily to settle in. She called her students and arranged class times for all of them.

The doors on a cuckoo clock in the living room clicked open as Lily held up the extra violin left behind for her by Kitty. Lily waited for the mechanical cuckoo bird to finish chirping twice before demonstrating the first few bars of a chaconne for Paoi. She didn't use her own violin when she taught because she found the slightly whiny tone of the instrument depressing. Paoi's mouth gaped open, as was her habit, while she observed her teacher's exaggerated vibrato.

"You try it now." Lily indicated the beginning of the solo on the music score with her bow and stood back, giving Paoi sufficient space. Once or twice Lily had been poked in the chin or chest by a student and had learned her lesson about keeping a safe distance.

Paoi struggled to find the right fingering and Lily occasionally played a note at the right pitch to give her a clue. Paoi was skinny—the kind of skinny that made bras unnecessary and garments hang loosely. Lily herself was not wearing a bra, either. She didn't like them. When she was in high school, her mother had bought her half a dozen bras off the clearance rack at the mall with absolutely no idea of her size. At some point Nina had taken all of these bras and thrown them into the big black trash can outside, a gesture that both frightened and moved Lily.

"You have lovely tits. Don't hide them," Nina said.

Covering one's breasts in Canada was hardly a concern, anyway, since everyone was so bundled up most of the time, layer upon layer.

Lily knew that the outline of her small breasts and perky nipples were apparent under almost every non-winter garment she owned, but she decided that it was no big deal, even though hers were possibly the only nipples visible on the streets of Taipei. Correction: hers were the only breasts not supported or covered by a bra that were not the sagging, wrinkled dugs of an *obasan* aged over sixty. Even her mother would have worn a bra, and would probably make her wear one too, had she been here.

When Paoi's hour was up, Lily sent her out to photocopy some scores at the 7-11 nearby and waited for the next student, Anya. Cute, round-faced Anya had dimpled hands that could move almost as fast as Lily's, but thankfully with less accuracy. This was the only student Lily had to practice for, whose pieces she had to rehearse before she demonstrated them for her in class. Anya's more difficult piece at this point was *Preludium and Allegro*, which Lily had played in fourth-grade but messed up horribly at the mid-semester music exams. Her violin teacher was embarrassed and furious at how Lily ruined an entire staccato passage by losing control of her bow, which made whistling and bumping noises while touching only fifty percent of the correct strings for a full minute. Despite the hopelessness of her right hand, her left hand kept pressing the notes on the fingerboard, to little effect. Mrs. Gu later told her that everyone said the judges at the exam were mouthing to one another, *Whose student is this?* and, *Maybe we should stop her.*

Images of her fourth-grade exam passed through Lily's head as she and Anya played. Just like ten-year-old Lily, Anya couldn't do the *Allegro*. Lily showed her how to bounce the bow and control it with a thumb and forefinger, maintaining the bow's balance with her pinky. Finally, Anya managed a few successful staccatos and Lily praised her profusely, marking out the entire section as next week's homework, a great compliment. It was an insult when the teacher only marked out a few bars for next week, one Lily had often received and resented, even when she knew she deserved it because she rarely practiced at home.

While Anya put on her shoes at the front door, Anya's mother stared blatantly at Lily's breasts, their outline visible through her thin T-shirt. The woman's glance said it all: *wear a bra—you're indecent*. Then she told her son, who was supposed to be Lily's four o'clock, to wait outside.

"I meant to tell your aunt this, but my son will be very busy at school preparing for the entrance exam for college, so I think we'll take a break from lessons until the exams are over. I'm sure you understand, Miss Gu." Her icy voice seemed mismatched with her intensely crimson lipstick. Some of the lipstick was on her teeth.

"Why, of course," Lily said, forcing herself to look at the woman's eyes instead of her teeth.

The boy turned back to glance at Lily and was given a warning shove by his mother.

Lily wondered if it was just her imagination that Anya's mom had been offended by her braless breasts. Surely one doesn't lose music students over this kind of thing. She knew Taiwanese were weird about nipples, but she didn't have to be like them, acting all ashamed of the female body.

On her way to and from the supermarket, in the streets, Lily started searching for white women, hoping to see one without a bra on, to prove she wasn't alone and wasn't crazy. She saw a few foreign tourists, but their ample breasts were all well-contained and covered, as were their nipples.

A month and a half later, only Paoi and the adult male student remained on Lily's schedule. Anya, soon after her brother, was crossed out from Kitty's old schedule, but

Paoi and Guo Sun came loyally, weekly, to Lily's apartment, scratching out on squeaky violins their tone-deaf tunes in the living room. Fortunately for the neighbors, this room had been soundproofed by the previous tenant, an aspiring singer who practiced karaoke every night. White boards covered with tiny holes like tunnels made by worms surrounding the room sucked in most of the awful attempts at music within.

Paoi's mother had been discreetly increasing the amount of money she gave Lily, an undiscussed but much appreciated raise of a hundred NT every month or so. By now, when Paoi handed Lily an envelope after class, it contained twelve hundred NT. Guo Sun, who earned his own tuition, didn't give Lily extra money, and sometimes forgot the tuition, but he always tried the best he could as a boring Taiwanese engineer to make conversation with her.

Occasionally they went out after class to have sweet dumplings from a food stall or a cup of boba tea. Guo Sun never let Lily see the bill, quoting Confucius, "If anything is needed by the teacher, the student will naturally be of service." Lily let him pay since she figured he owed her tuition anyway.

Today Paoi was supposed to come at 1:30 p.m., but she failed to show up. Around four o'clock, Lily picked up the phone and spoke to Mrs. Wu, Paoi's mother, who was speaking in an apologetic tone. Paoi was falling behind academically, she said, and she had no choice but to have her take a break from violin lessons for now.

"I understand," Lily said.

"Thank you so much for teaching my daughter, Teacher Gu." Mrs. Gu sounded guilty and hung up right away after a few polite goodbyes.

Lily knew Paoi and Anya's moms were good friends. Anya's mom must have persuaded Paoi's mother not to let her daughter take lessons from a braless, indecent Taiwanese-Canadian woman—Lily was sure of it. Taiwan was so screwed up. It was too bad. Lily didn't mind Paoi as a student, and she actually liked Paoi's mom. She admired her elegant clothes and rose-scented perfume. Her modest rack was no doubt covered in a thick designer bra with extra molding for protection and supported with underwire.

This left Lily with just one student, the tone-deaf engineer who bought her sweet dumplings after class. So much for making her own living; her father would still have to wire her money for rent. But at least this time it would be from one Taipei bank to another instead of all the way from Taipei to Canada, with all the banks in between helping themselves to foreign exchange and transaction fees.

To clear her head, Lily took a walk around her neighborhood and found herself with a craving for a savory rice triangle wrapped in nori. Luckily there was a 7-11 every few blocks, so she would likely find her favorite type of rice triangle, wasabi salmon. As she walked along the betel-nut-juice-stained sidewalk with a new sense of purpose, she noticed a stranger trying to keep up with her, several paces away from her on the sidewalk. Instinctively, she quickened her pace.

The man addressed her, "Miss, miss!"

Lily stopped. Maybe she had dropped something and he was a good Samaritan. She turned around to see a short man whose head only reached her ear.

"Miss, may I beg you to wear a bra, please?"

Lily stared at the little man, whose silver-rimmed glasses framed his beady eyes. A striped shirt stretched over his paunch, and a worn belt held up his cheap suit pants.

"Please wear a . . . bra under your shirt. It's really obvious." He was looking into her face, clearly trying as hard as he could to look away from her breasts, which were closer to him.

Lily whipped her head back around and marched away, fuming. Who did this stupid shrimp think he was, acting like she was indecent? She wanted to swear a hundred curses at him, but not knowing what else to do, she fled. She felt like a weakling, a coward. What would Nina have said in such a situation? She would have known what to do. Forget talk—Nina would have beaten the little man up.

Eight o'clock Sunday evening, Guo Sun arrived five minutes early for his lesson. Lily gave him two new three-octave scales and arpeggios to fumble through as warm up. As he played she tried not to think about the horrible little man who told her to wear a bra, but every bad note the engineer hit reminded her of those perverted, beady eyes and the man's condescending tone.

"Do you mind terribly if we skip class today? We could go out for some iced tea." Lily interrupted Guo Sun in the middle of an arpeggio.

"Sure, the student is always at the teacher's service."

In under five minutes, he gathered his music books, loosened his bow hair and stuffed everything into his violin case.

At the tea house, Lily sipped black tea while Guo Sun stirred his frothy pearl milk green tea, sucking tapioca balls at an impressive speed through a thick straw.

"Is something the matter?" Guo Sun asked.

"I ran into this pervert yesterday." Lily stirred the ice in furious circles in her tea.

"I'm sorry to hear that. That's what a big city is like, I guess. My cousin also has had such experiences. She calls the perverts *weird uncles*. My cousin is quite cute. Are you okay? Did the pervert say something to you?"

"He followed me for a while and came up to me and told me to wear . . . a bra."

The corners of Guo Sun's lips curled upwards slightly. He seemed to be suppressing a smile. "I hope you don't mind my saying so, Teacher Gu, but yeah, it might help if you did wear one."

"Excuse me?" Lily stabbed her straw into the ice and glared at Guo Sun, almost as angry at him as she was at the little man in the street.

"Please don't be offended. I mean, you know what Taiwanese are like. Some men can be sleazy, and the women will talk, too. You can't let them see too much of your body. People see, and people talk."

Lily couldn't believe her ears. "I think I need to go home now."

"Please don't go. Are you angry?"

Guo Sun reached out and touched her right hand, which she drew back.

"You know, Lily, I mean, Teacher Gu, you are one of the most talented girls I know. I want to tell you that. I . . . rather like you. I don't care about the bra thing. Not one bit. You look great. Other people are idiots."

Lily stood up and headed to the door. She didn't feel like explaining anything to Guo Sun: that he didn't have the right to discuss her body or her bra, that she didn't like him like that, and never would. Lily left him in the tea house without looking back. He was too polite and also too stunned to chase after her.

He had been her last violin student.

And then there were none.

Had she lost each and every one of her students because she refused to wear a bra, because even perverted, dumpling-shaped, strange men in the streets of Taipei were offended by the contour of her nipples? Lily felt more confused than ever, and insulted. Maybe she was wrong. Despite Nina's angry voice protesting in her mind, Lily wondered whether it was time to buy one of those thickly-padded, lacy Taiwanese bras.

Betel Nut Beauty

TAKE THE ARECA nut, marinated in milk and dried in the sun, and cut it open. Stuff a ball of fibers made from flowers from a betel plant between the cheeks of the open nut. Wrap it in a betel leaf folded in half, stem removed, smeared with some red-brownish goop that looks like dirty blood. Then you have a betel nut, Taiwanese-style. It looks exactly like a vagina, a round, crisp, green one with a humongous rust-colored, hooded clitoris.

I didn't always have to prepare and sell betel nuts. I used to have a better life, and certainly deserved one.

I see Moli, sitting at the betel nut stand in a lime-green T-shirt and knee-length white skirt, talking on the cell phone with that no-good boyfriend of hers again.

"Aw, really? But I wanted to go . . . okay, fine. Tomorrow night. Keep your promise, Feng!"

She hangs up with a pout, and my heart hurts for her.

She's my oldest daughter and I named her after the jasmine flower. Even a flower has more self-esteem than her, letting a man play her like that. I've told her so many times to dump him.

I walk up to her and hand her a bag of betel plant leaves.

"He's married," I say. "It's no use. And have you forgotten your father? How he ran off with a little tart and left us to make a living selling these dirty *bin-lang*?"

"Don't talk about it like it's my fault," Moli mutters beneath her breath.

Haili, the younger one, doesn't say anything, and pretends not to hear her sister or see my anger. She only folds a stuffed areca nut into a fresh green leaf and puts it into a small paper box.

Our betel nut stand has little Christmas lights around it and a transparent refrigerator case to keep the prepared betel nuts fresh. The stand faces an alley that turns away from and back to a main road, a good location for our business. This isn't one of the better neighborhoods in Taipei, as my husband bought the apartment when he first started his job after law school and didn't have much money. He promised we would move to a bigger, nicer place after Haili was born, but soon after we brought her back from the hospital, he ran off with a little tart. He lives in a grand house in the scenic mountains with that woman while we squat here in this ugly apartment with a betel nut stand in front of it, surrounded by open sewers that stink and sidewalks stained by dog shit and juice from garbage and betel nuts.

I should have been a well-dressed, leisurely lady who shopped in department stores and had afternoon tea with friends instead of squatting behind this *bin-lang* stand, peeling betel leaves apart, mixing lime tar with my daughters. A poem of mine won a classical Chinese poetry contest in high school, but now I manage a betel nut stand. My ex-husband hid away all his money so his little secretary could buy a house under her name, and by the time we were divorced, my girls and I got barely anything. He was a lawyer and knew all the tricks of family courts in Taiwan; I had no means to hire a good lawyer to fight back, not to mention he knew the judge personally.

I brought these girls up on my own.

I tell them from my own experience what men are like. And do they listen? No.

Moli used to be so chubby. Look at her now, a stick figure. One summer she decided to lose weight, and she just kept losing, losing. She'd scream at me if I made her eat some real food; she only chewed gum, ate green grapes, and drank winter melon tea all day.

Her deft fingers are wrapping betel nuts and putting them in little boxes. She and her sister, Haili, go through the motions during the slow time of day between one and two in the afternoon while I watch them from my seat in the back and balance our accounts. I keep an eye on the customers so those dirty men don't put their salty pig hands on my daughters. My girls deserve better.

We all deserve better.

Lam brings me some tea. I smile at him.

Lam is a neighbor's son. His family moved out of town a few years ago, but he stayed here for his job. He's been sleeping on our sofa for years; he's like my adopted son. He helps around the house and is like a big brother to my daughters, being a good seven, eight years older than them.

I like having a man around the house. I feel less like a sad, divorced *obasan*, an old bag. Lam is a great comfort to me. I never had a son, but he is almost better than my own children—he's giving, considerate, and always listens to what I have to say.

A man calls to Haili and Moli, "*Bin-lang Si Se!*" as he passes by on a scooter. Si Se was one of the most beautiful women in Chinese history, but the way he says *bin-lang Si Se*, 'betel nut beauty,' is leering, and I glare at him. He's a betel nut addict, you can tell from his teeth that are black from the stuffing in betel nuts and his loose gums. The mouths of most of our regulars look like this.

"I'm sorry, Ma, don't be angry," he calls in my direction, turning back to buy a box of betel nuts.

At the stand, Haili accepts his crumpled one hundred-NT bill and hands him a box.

My girls, seventeen and nineteen, are pretty in their own ways. But if they were any prettier I wouldn't let them work at this stand—it's too dangerous. Moli, almost model-like, is much taller than Haili, who is my size, about 155 centimeters.

People often say jokingly that I can sit at the *bin-lang* stand myself because I look youthful, like my daughters' big sister, with the same upward-pointed phoenix eyes. It's nice of them to say that of an *obasan* like me. My skin is sallow, unlike the nice cream color when I was younger; I have crow's feet, bags under my eyes, and I have to dye my hair to hide the gray. I haven't gained an ounce since I got married, though, and from the backside I could pass as twenty-five, still, if it weren't for my hairstyle—short permed hair that is the fashion for middle-aged Taiwanese women, to hide the hair loss that comes with age.

We eat lunch separately but dinner together. Lam often cooks for us because he's a brilliant chef—my favorite is his soy-cooked pig feet and stir-fried squid, both of which he made tonight. I fill an extra large bowl of rice for him to show my gratitude and a large bowl for myself to show my appreciation.

"Pig feet again? Not me," Moli says and puts down her chopsticks. "I'm sick of even the smell of them, ugh. And it's all fat. Fat makes my skin break out."

Haili picks up some vegetables with her chopsticks and puts them on her rice in silence. Whenever her older sister is being hostile, she takes her side automatically.

Lam takes a bite out of a piece of squid at his corner of the table, head lowered. I feel bad for him. My girls have been more and more cruel to both him and me as they've grown. Adolescent girls are so ungrateful.

Moli puts an almost untouched bowl of rice back in the kitchen. Her sister follows her, and I hear the two of them speaking in low voices in the kitchen. I only catch fragments of their conversation.

"I thought he canceled—"

"I'm going anyway . . . to his house, I don't care—"

"But he might get mad—"

"I have the right to—"

"I don't know, Moli—"

"It's really none of your business—"

They wash their bowls and chopsticks noisily so that I cannot hear most of what they say. Soon Moli goes back to her room, and Haili comes back to the table, peeling an orange.

Fifteen minutes later, Moli emerges in the figure-hugging floral dress she bought herself for her birthday, wearing makeup, sparkly blush and unnaturally blue eye shadow. She must have used so much blue powder for it to show on our skin tone. I don't like to see her with powder on her face; it makes her look artificial and shallow.

"I'm going out," she announces, one high-heeled sandal already out the door.

"Where are you going?" I ask.

"Out." She slams the door.

"What's wrong with your sister, Haili?" I ask my remaining daughter.

"Dunno," she says, and stuffs her mouth with a piece of orange.

Later at night, I sit alone in the living room, mixing the stuffing for betel nuts. Most of the ingredients come in plastic bags, and I have to combine them in the right proportion: camphor, tobacco, nutmeg, clove, saffron, musk, coconut, fennel, gray-amber, and turmeric. Lam is scrubbing the kitchen and bathrooms, something he does almost every other day. Our floors and wall tiles are always spotless. I can hear the eight o'clock soap opera on the television from Haili and Moli's room; at least Haili is still a good girl and stays at home, unlike her big sister.

In the middle of the night, I am awakened by Haili's and Moli's voices. Moli sounds like she is crying.

I open the door and see my two girls hugging each other on Moli's bed.

"What's wrong?" I ask.

Moli sees me, wipes her tears with the back of her hand, and screws her face into a scowl. When I see her face my mouth drops open. Beneath her left eye, red and swollen from crying, is a purple and red bruise that nearly reaches her cheekbone.

"What did that animal do to you?" I reach toward her but she jerks away.

"None of your business!" Moli screams in a hoarse voice. She must have already been yelling before this.

"Ma— " Haili says, "Now is not a good time."

"Not a good time? When is it a good time? When your sister finally gets beaten to a pulp by that no-good, cheating bastard? When will you girls learn?"

I am close to tears. I cannot bear the thought of my poor daughter being hit by a good-for-nothing man. My girls get hit by nobody. Even their father never raised his hand to them when he was around.

"It's all your fault!" Moli cries, convulsing. "You made me work in this disgusting *bin-lang* stand. You ruined my life. He called me a dirty *bin-lang Si Se* and he says he doesn't want to see me again!"

The air around me feels ice cold, but my face is burning. "You are not dirty, you are not a dirty *bin-lang Si Se*, you hear that? I will tell that man how wrong he is. I will show him. You are good girls, my girls, it's not like you're working in the transparent betel nut booths next to the highway, exposing yourselves like prostitutes. You are not that! You are good girls, do you hear me? There is nothing wrong with what you do. That man is a bastard; he is wrong!"

"I don't care, you ruined my life! You hypocritical bitch! You talk about how horrible men are, that they cheat, prefer younger women. You are worse than all of them put together! You think we don't know about Lam? You think we don't know that he sneaks into your bedroom at night? I'm sick of you pretending you are a perfect mother. You are such a fake!"

I slap Moli; I cannot help it. I slap her twice: once on her face, once on her shoulder as she turns. She is so much taller that I almost lose my balance after the impact.

Haili forces her way between us, crying.

"Stop it, stop it, Mom, the two of you, stop fighting. Stop talking like that, Moli—"

"No, you know what, I've had enough of your silence, Haili. You know everything they do and you have no guts to say anything about it except to me. You're the one who told me about the noises you heard from your wall years ago, the noise of our mother being a huge disgusting whore! And now I hear it all the time, you're the one who made me realize what was going on and there you are standing there with that look on your face, like you're *oh-so-surprised*, you're almost as bad as her—"

I sink into Haili's bed, tears flowing. Haili looks at her sister with a frightened expression on her face. I see Lam's figure in the doorway. He heard the crying and screaming. He must have heard every piercing word from Moli. I want to fall into his arms, but can't, not in front of my daughters. They have made me feel dirty. None of this is my fault. I told Moli not to date a married man. But she was stupid and wouldn't listen. I warned her, didn't I? It isn't my fault, I am a good mother . . .

Writing on the Basement Wall

*T*HERE IS A *Chinese superstition that those who commit suicide wearing red clothes will become powerful, vengeful ghosts. They will come back and seek retribution for the injury done to them when they were still alive.*

Cynthia woke up late. Fortunately, Han Lin Vocational College enforced a strict uniform code, so she did not have to rummage through her closet looking for a cute outfit. She did, however, search for a pair of long, white socks since short, calf-exposing ones were considered indecent by the president, Mrs. Lin.

The radio blasted static-y news on ICRT, the only English radio station based in Taipei. The good thing about listening to the station, although Cynthia's listening comprehension only allowed her to pick up phrases here or there, was that it broadcast strictly international or political news. No horrible Taiwanese society news about the man who stabbed his ex-girlfriend last night or the love suicide of the daughter of Taipei's premier hypnotist. No acid poured on anyone's face, no stalkers, kidnappers, gangsters, sex crimes.

Finally dressed and ready for school, Cynthia rushed out of the apartment. When she turned around to lock her door, she noticed a piece of paper taped onto its exterior.

Dear tenant:
a message in red mentioning your name was found scribbled on the basement wall. As much as we regret this, we must ask you to take full responsibility for cleaning the writing on the wall as soon as possible, as it must be left by an acquaintance of yours.
The Building Manager, No.3 Sing Yi Street.

Cynthia crumpled the note and avoided eye contact with the building manager at his desk as she walked hastily out of the front entrance of her ugly tile building. At the bus stop, she tossed the paper ball, now a tight, warm wad, into a wastebasket.

The sun's last rays turned everything a burnt, golden color as Cynthia dragged her heavy feet through the front gate of her building again after school. She had no idea what went on in class all day; she drifted from classroom to classroom like a phantom.

No one sat at the front desk in the lobby. The building manager was too old to be of any use as a guard—had been for over a decade. Her downstairs neighbor, old Mrs. Yeh, had told her how in 1984 a bunch of robbers came in, held a gun to the manager's head, and carried out over twenty bicycles right before his eyes.

"That was back when bicycles were actually worth something. When we asked the building manager how he could just let them take everything, he said, *they had a thing.*" Mrs. Yeh made the shape of a gun with her right hand.

If more robbers came and held guns to the building manager's head, it would serve him right, Cynthia thought. As she ascended the stairs, she heard something behind her. She turned to see the shadow of a man in the stairway entrance. A middle-aged stranger emerged before her, his eyes round, maniacal, left hand holding a knife in a manner ready to stab. The gleam from the knife in the dim staircase contrasted with the dark stairs leading to the basement. She ran upstairs, up two stories, three, hearing the man's footsteps always half a flight beneath her.

When she reached the seventh floor of the building, she saw that the door of an apartment facing the staircase was open. She rushed into the apartment, shut the metal door, and pulled the lock and chain in place. Turning around, she surveyed the apartment, heart still racing. Chinese scrolls, seashells, and upside-down, desiccated flowers decorated the cabinets. Most of the furniture was wicker or bamboo. Cynthia tread softly into the living room, rolling her feet from heel to toe. She saw an old woman, shriveled and hunched with age, watering plants with a spray hose on the balcony crowded with potted plants. When the old woman stepped in and closed the screen door after her, Cynthia approached.

"Excuse me, *Po Po*."

The old woman gave her a broad grin: all gums, no teeth. Her wrinkled lips looked like bleached prunes. "You must be Yune's friend. Welcome, welcome."

"I'm sorry. I don't know anyone in your family. I live in your building and—"

The old woman put her hand on Cynthia's shoulder and interrupted, "I don't have my hearing aid, darling. It broke last week. You just wait here, Yune will be back from school soon. I'm going into the kitchen to make dinner. Make yourself at home." She wiped her hands on her floral patterned pants and shuffled into the kitchen.

Cynthia didn't know what to do. She peered through the cloudy peep hole in the door: the hallway was empty. She was about to sit down on a bamboo rocking chair when the old woman appeared again, holding a plate of sliced mango.

"Here, have some fruit."

Cynthia stood, unsure of what to do. She wanted to tell the woman she shouldn't have gone to the trouble of peeling and cutting up mangos, that she didn't know Yune, and she didn't feel like eating fruit because a stranger had just come after her with a gleaming knife. But the woman could hear nothing, so instead Cynthia nodded graciously and accepted the plate.

She heard the sizzle of moist vegetables landing in a wok coming from the kitchen. She picked up a piece of mango with a toothpick and put it in her mouth. It tasted treacly, over-ripe. She pushed the other pieces on the plate aside, creating an empty space, making it look like she had taken more pieces and had appreciated the hostess's efforts. Then, slipping the toothpick into her uniform skirt pocket, she left, closing the door behind her.

He was Cynthia's first boyfriend. They met under unremarkable circumstances. She was on her way to the stationery store for manila envelopes, and he stopped her to ask what time it was, leaning down from his motorcycle. In the following weeks she gave him more than her time—all her firsts besides her virginity. Once or twice they went to a motel and rubbed against each other's bodies, and she watched or helped him finish, but she never let things get further than that. He was discontent, and things between them began going south.

When Cynthia asked for a break-up, he threatened to kill himself. He would write a suicide note, he said. The note would instruct his gangster parents to kill Cynthia, the girl who made their only son take his own life, and they would. And then they would kill her family. He sent her letters written in his own blood, the ugly handwriting bleeding shades of orange and rust on paper crinkled from the uneven drying of blood. He followed her after school, once or twice pushing her into construction sites near her campus and feeling her up savagely.

Cynthia's father knew nothing—he did not notice that his daughter never left the house during the weekend without his company. He did not see that she had picked at and bitten her nails until they were so short and broken they cracked and bled.

This continued all winter and spring. In the summer, Cynthia went south to stay with her paternal grandparents.

When classes began again in March, Cynthia's stalker was gone. She still never felt entirely safe, and wished she had friends at school. She was just one of the faceless many wearing the same uniforms and hairstyle at Han Lin Vocational School. Nobody knew her, and ultimately, nobody would notice when she was killed by her ex-boyfriend's parents, her insane ex, or a middle-aged stranger with crazy eyes and a sharp knife in the basement.

The morning after receiving the awful note, after a broken night's sleep, Cynthia finally trudged downstairs in her slippers and pajamas to look at the writing on the basement wall.

Cynthia you heartless Bitch I am going to Cut Slice your heart OUT just like you did mine You Just Wait

Cynthia put one palm against the horrible wall to support herself. The message was scrawled in either red paint or blood in his crazed handwriting. He was back. She wished they had never met. She would be the next headline in the Taiwan news, she could see it: "Vocational School Student Brutally Mutilated by Spurned Boyfriend." The old woman on the seventh floor would open the newspaper, read about her and say, "Why, that's just awful," as she sipped the cup of tea her granddaughter Yune brought to her. Cynthia's grandparents would sob and blame their son for not bringing her up right, for letting her live alone in dangerous Taipei when her thoughtless mother had already abandoned her as a baby. They would lament the fate of their nineteen-year-old granddaughter, too young and innocent to meet such a horrible end.

Cynthia walked stiffly back up to her apartment. She combed her hair, washed her face, put on a bright red dress she wore to a wedding last year, and eased her feet into a pair of red ballet flats. She turned on all the lights in her apartment and switched the radio to ICRT.

Instead of going down to the first floor, she took the elevator to the twelfth floor. She climbed up a staircase which led to the roof of the building. A jungle of gas and satellite equipment lined the flat, cement roof. A large water tower hummed in its metal net. She stepped over some ailing plants in cracked pots and made her way between rows of clothes drying on bamboo poles fixed in place with stacked bricks. Cynthia gazed down at the rest of Taipei through a layer of moist morning smog. The sun malingered behind clouds.

She approached the waist-high ledge, leaned on it with trembling hands, and closed her eyes for several seconds.

She put one red shoe on the ledge, then with a boost, the other. She didn't take the time to rebalance herself as she stood, and she simply fell, fell, and landed on the first floor, in an unswept alley beside No.3 Sing Yi Street.

A neighbor's dog barked, hearing the dull thump of the body.

My Ex-Boyfriend the Spy

IN THE BASEMENT of a popular Taipei gym, two young women wrapped in nothing but plush white towels sat side by side on the wooden bench in a sauna room. Their eyes were half closed as they leaned back in the small space saturated with hot steam.

"It's so hot I can't breathe," Angela said.

"You'll get used to it. Relax."

An older woman left, leaving Angela and May alone in the room. May moved to the bench where the older woman had been lying, removed her towel, spread it lengthwise on the bench, and lay down on it. She crossed her legs in Angela's direction. Angela gazed idly at her friend's naked body, slender with rounded breasts, the lower body slightly thick.

"How long has it been since a guy saw you naked?" Angela asked, observing the curved outline of May's breasts.

May laughed. "It's been a while. It's not exactly convenient to have a boyfriend when you're living at home. I'm almost thirty, but my gramps still watches me like a hawk. How about your parents?"

"Mine don't really care. They're too busy running the supermarket. They don't bother me even if I come home late," Angela said.

"Have you dated anyone since you broke up with Dennis?"

"No. But hey, at least I didn't forget his name this time."

"You loose woman, sleeping with men whose names you don't know!"

Angela's face reddened, but at least she could blame it on the steam. "Hey, watch it. That was my first boyfriend."

"The older guy? Where the hell do you find these old men, anyway?"

"I ran into him a few times on campus and had asked his name twice but still forgot it. By the time he finally convinced me to go out with him, I could not for the life of me remember his name, and a few dates later, it was too embarrassing to ask him."

"So how *did* you find out his name?"

"We were lying in bed in a motel room one afternoon, and I suddenly had a brilliant idea. I asked him what his friends called him, and he said Will. So I knew his name must be Will or William, and I could just call him Will."

"Just how old was he?"

"I never asked him his age, but he must have been over forty."

"How old were you?"

"Nineteen."

"That's nasty." May made a face.

"Well, I didn't think too hard about it. He was really weird and secretive, though. He always invited me on remote hiking trails outside of Taipei, and I never knew his telephone number or address. He always called me. I never called him."

"That sounds really shady," May said.

"Well, when I told my next boyfriend, the Irish guy, about how secretive Will was, he was certain that Will was some kind of spy working for the American government."

"Spy? That's ridiculous. I'm sorry, but that sounds paranoid and crazy. Why on earth would America need spies in Taiwan? Taiwanese love Americans."

"I thought it seemed odd, too."

"You want to know what I think, Angela?"

"Enlighten me."

"He was married," May said with conviction.

"Married?"

"Yes, that's the most logical and obvious explanation."

"Hmm, he did used to check the motel rooms for hidden cameras, which I thought was funny. Who cares if perverted motel owners got our naked butts on film? He said he wanted to protect me because I was so young. And he always, always insisted on using a condom and didn't allow me to even touch him without one already on."

"So there you go; he was married, simple as that. No spy conspiracy theories, nothing psycho or paranoid," May said.

Angela's face grew dark, and she felt herself sweating profusely, not just because of the heat. She felt nauseous and lightheaded. Perhaps it had occurred to her that Will might have been married, but she'd subconsciously blocked the possibility out, even after all the years. This was the man who took her virginity, the first man she was ever serious about, and it turns out he was only having her on the side, that he was married the whole time? Angela felt something snapping inside her.

"When I asked him where he lived, he said he lived with a Taiwanese family. I thought it was a language exchange type of setup." Angela clenched her teeth.

"Maybe that's a euphemism for *I live with my wife and kids*," May said. "Yep, the asshole was *so* married."

"He's such a piece of shit!" Angela burst out. "I gave him my first time, my first everything! And I can't believe it took five years after we broke up for me to figure this out."

"Calm down, it's okay, it's all in the past. I mean, what are you going to do?"

"I'd like to slap him hard and tell him off," Angela said.

"How are you going to find him if you don't have his address?"

"I don't know. Maybe I can go hang out on the Taida campus and see if he's still there trying to pick up young college girls."

"Come on. Let's go in the cold water pool to cool off," May said, getting up from the bench and rewrapping her towel around her body. "You're getting way too worked up."

The two women exited the sauna. In the adjoining room, they plunged into the coolness of the tile-lined cold water pool.

"Wow, my skin feels all prickly," Angela said.

"It's nice, isn't it? Feel better now?"

The next day, Angela spent her lunch hour on the Taida campus at the cafeteria benches, where she had run into Will many times five years ago. May would've told her to give it up if she knew Angela was stupidly waiting here in hopes of running into her ex to tell him off for being married and stringing her along, but this was just one of those things. Angela needed this. That she had inadvertently dated a married man, and that he had told her how much he loved her and actually wept, a grown man weeping like a baby when she came back from studying abroad in Europe for a year and dumped him—all of this made her angry. The more she thought about it, the more she fumed.

Sure, she had had the satisfaction of dumping him when she came back with the much younger boyfriend she replaced him with, but that was nothing compared to her new knowledge that he had a family. He would never be able to make amends for this insult, this injury, this wrongdoing, done to her as well as his wife.

She started eating lunch on the Taida campus daily. She bought lunch at the cafeteria, just like she did five years ago as an undergraduate, and ate it on the open benches beside the bike racks. It was like she was back in college again. The excellent food options had not changed much since she was there, and she enjoyed the variety—cold sesame noodles, steamed buns, sticky rice with chicken and tea eggs, delicious fried chicken patties, beef noodle soup, and savory pork meatball soup.

One whole year passed before Angela caught a glimpse of a tall, gray-haired man on a bicycle. She had reduced her visits from five days a week to one or two days a week, starting to believe she would never see him again.

The man locked his bike to the bicycle rack by the road, and when Angela saw his face, she froze. She dropped her steamed bun and stood.

He hadn't seen her yet. She took large strides toward him. He had an envelope in his hand and was walking toward the post office. There were so many people coming and going in the plaza that he didn't notice her. Without thinking, Angela cut in front of him and blocked his path. She watched as his pupils dilated with recognition and disbelief.

"Angela, it's you! I thought I would never see you again! How are you?"

"I would be better if you had told me the truth about yourself," she said.

She crossed her arms and tapped the right toe of her high-heeled shoes. When Will knew her, she wore sneakers, old jeans, and tank tops. Now she wore a nice blouse, fitted office pants, and expensive high heels with pointy toes as sharp as weapons. She wanted to dig them into his gut.

"What do you mean, the truth?"

"You know exactly what I mean. You're married, aren't you?"

"I'm not married now," he said, dragging out each syllable the way liars do.

"But were you married then? When you fucked me and told me you loved me and cried when I was leaving and then cried when I dumped you? When I gave you my virginity? You were married, weren't you, you piece of shit!"

"I . . . calm down, Angela, I didn't mean to—"

"Answer my question!" she yelled, though all the Taida students nearby were staring, some gawping mid-chew, at the two of them.

She wasn't a student here anymore, anyway. She did not care. Nobody she knew was here to gossip about her, and all she wanted was to make Will feel shame, as he had made her feel when she realized how naïve and stupid she had been to believe him and trust him.

"Yes, I was married," Will said softly, "but I got divorced shortly after you and I broke up."

"See if I care."

"When I told you that I would have married you, I was sincere. I wanted to marry you. I really loved you," he said quietly.

Angela tried not to let the old man's words affect her. Marry her, indeed. Who wanted to marry him? She stared right in his face and was surprised to see what an old, graying, long-faced, and unattractive creature he was. She could not believe she had been naked in bed with this man, given him her affection, offered him her body. She really dodged a bullet, she thought to herself. When he opened his mouth he showed two rows of undoubtedly fake teeth so shiny and blindingly white they looked frightening against his receded, reddish-pink gums. Angela's feelings toward Will shifted from anger to a kind of pity, which soon gave way to disgust.

"Get away from me. You don't deserve to have anyone in your life, you dirty old liar. If I could take everything back, I would."

The expression on Will's face triggered in Angela the vivid image of her twisting a knife in his wound so it would never heal. But it was still not enough.

"You are a piece of shit, human scum, and I shouldn't have wasted a single minute on you. I regret every second I spent with you, and I'm sure your ex-wife does, too."

Will stood there, pruny mouth stretched into a flat line of dismay. Angela turned and started walking, her heels clicking loudly on the sidewalk. She walked toward the bus stop at the front gate of Taida. She imagined Will was following her, a mere arm's reach away as she crossed the crowded campus, but she refused to look back. As she approached the bus stop, her bus, the number 60 Taipei bus, pulled up. She waved at the driver and quickened her steps, making it just in time. The door of the bus swung shut behind her with a whooshing noise. She dropped twelve NT into the coin chute and plopped down in the first seat behind the driver.

Angela looked out the window at the familiar Taipei scenery: couples on bicycles, mothers with strollers, elementary school students wearing school uniforms and banana-yellow hats. A sense of satisfaction and vindication flowed through her. At last, she had the closure she wanted. She only wished she had remembered to slap him while she was at it. Fishing her cell phone out of her purse, she dialed May's number. She hadn't spoken to May since her friend began a demanding new job answering telephones for a home shopping network. Even when May wasn't busy, she no longer enjoyed talking on the phone—"occupational hazard," she jokingly explained.

"Hey, May, you won't believe who I just ran into," she said when May picked up.

Simple as That

SHE THOUGHT IT was a matter of being a wonderful, loving girlfriend who could cook, looked pretty, and had a nice body. All she had to do, or be, were these things, and love him, and he would love her back, as simple as that. She was wrong.

She met him by chance in the lobby of a karaoke club. He spoke to her in perfect Chinese, which took her by surprise, because his eyes were sapphire and his hair dark auburn.

"Are you waiting for me?" he asked.

Jolie did not understand this as a pick-up line, only stared at him, confused.

"It was a joke," he said. "Hi, my name is Mike."

"I'm Jolie."

Jolie wasn't in the mood for chatting, especially since she had just broken up with her long-distance boyfriend after he admitted he had been with two different girls behind her back and still expected her to forgive him. She didn't, and was feeling rather sore about men in general. This was why she wanted to go to karaoke with the girls—so they could bitch about men and sing sad love songs by Tsai Chin until they lost their voices. But politeness forced her to keep up a conversation with Mike until her friends arrived.

"You speak Chinese very well," she said to him. "Everybody must say that to you."

"Yeah, and guess what, I speak English very well, too. I just came here after graduating from college in America. I majored in Chinese." He smiled, showing perfect teeth.

"You have no accent when you speak Chinese," Jolie said.

"My nanny was from Taiwan," Mike said. "My parents were never around, so after school I would hang out with her and speak Chinese. I was like her son. I always told myself I would come to Taiwan when I had a chance."

"Where is your nanny now?"

"She got married to an American soldier when I was in sixth grade, and we kind of lost touch. At first, she wrote some letters and I wrote her back, but after a while there were no more letters, and I wasn't sure of her address anymore."

"That's too bad."

"Sometimes, I wonder if she got divorced and moved back to Taiwan. Maybe I'll find her again here."

"Why would you want her to be divorced?" Jolie thought Mike rather unkind to have such a fantasy.

"I'm just saying it's a possibility."

At that moment, Jolie realized that her two girlfriends, Yoyi and Angel, were spying on her and the red-headed foreigner through the glass lobby door. They giggled and looked guilty as they waved at Jolie. They walked in, wearing identical sly grins.

"Hi, Jolie, are we interrupting something?" Yoyi asked.

Jolie wanted to warn them not to say anything inappropriate or rude because this foreigner could understand Chinese perfectly, but she didn't have a chance.

"Good to see you've found a better man, dear, he's very cute," Angel said.

"Did you get his number?" Yoyi asked.

"Oh, stop it, you two, let's go," Jolie said, blushing fiercely.

Mike did not say anything, just smiled good-naturedly at the three girls.

"Hi," Yoyi said to Mike in English.

"Hi," Mike replied in English.

Then, seeing that Jolie had already darted into the elevator and Angel was just behind her, Yoyi said a hasty "Bye!" to Mike and ran after her friends.

Eight months later, Jolie was living with Mike in his apartment next to National Taiwan Normal University. They were a picture of domestic bliss. She worked part-time in a flower shop and spent half her day shopping for groceries and making nice dinners. Mike taught English at a cram school near Danshui and took the MRT back and forth every day. Some nights, when traffic was bad or he got waylaid by eager female students with post-lecture questions, he would not get home until eight or eight-thirty at night. Jolie felt like a genuine housewife those nights, trying to keep her dinner from becoming soggy or dried-out or cold while she waited dutifully. She loved Mike more than ever, and she was certain that he would propose to her any day now.

Sure, they had exchanged their "I love yous," or rather, Jolie was first to say, a few months into their dating, "I think I love you," while Mike, a few weeks after that, said to her, "I'm falling in love with you."

She never told her parents she was *cohabitating* with someone in Taipei City, which they considered the city of sin. But she hoped that after Mike proposed, she could legitimately introduce him to her parents as her fiancé, and everything would work out in the end, even if her parents scolded her a little for not telling them about him sooner.

A few days ago, however, Mike casually mentioned that he was taking the GRE so he could apply to graduate programs back in the United States. Jolie didn't know how to respond, because he had never mentioned graduate school or going back to America before. She cheered herself up by telling herself that, wherever he went, he would take her with him—after a romantic proposal, of course.

After thinking obsessively about their future marriage day and night for weeks, an email from an old classmate finally broke her. Mia, the most unlikely of her old friends to become a bride, was engaged. Mia, the most cynical misandrist on Earth, in love. Jolie hated that she was not happy for her old friend, but she was reminded of a line both Angel and Yoyi were fond of delivering, with all the dramatic flair of a Korean drama heroine: "Every time one of my friends gets engaged, I die a little bit inside."

Mia's engagement was the last straw.

Mike was watching a bag of butter popcorn pop in the microwave when Jolie said, quite abruptly and intensely, "You never mentioned you were planning to go to graduate school."

Mike appeared to be listening for the right interval between pops as a cue to turn off the microwave. He acted like he hadn't heard what she said.

"You know, Mike, I don't mean this as an ultimatum or anything like that, but if you really leave for America, there's no way for me to go there with you unless we're engaged or married."

Mike looked at Jolie as if a bat had just flown out of her mouth, but still, he said nothing.

"It's just that. Getting a long-term visa is very hard, I know from my friend's experience, and I'm not going to be a student at an American university or anything because I can't pass the TOEFL for English proficiency. I can't afford to come and go every three months on tourist visas because of the cost of airplane tickets, and—"

Jolie kept explaining until she sensed that Mike was no longer listening. His facial expression betrayed little, if any, emotion.

After a long silence, he said, "Okay. I get it. You don't have to keep harping about it."

Jolie felt hurt. She never considered herself someone who harped, and Mike's words made her feel like a shrew or a nagging woman. She realized she wasn't going to get a proposal out of Mike this way, at least not now. She didn't regret talking to him about it, however, because that was how she felt. And that wasn't even all of it.

When they were first dating, Mike took it upon himself to educate her about sexually transmitted diseases. Sex education in Taiwan wasn't particularly specific or comprehensive about the sexually transmitted diseases and sexually transmitted infections out there, so Jolie listened, wide-eyed, at times covering her mouth with her hands, at times shaking her head in disbelief, the whole time shuddering, while Mike went through the terms and symptoms. These STD/STI lectures began when the two of them got more intimate physically—nothing serious, just some kissing and touching.

"I wanted to educate you about all this because I have HPV," Mike said finally.

"That one is—"

"HPV is a virus that causes genital warts. It lives in your skin and doesn't go away. Where I have it cannot be covered by a condom, so basically if you have sexual contact with me, you will get the virus, too. It's mostly a cosmetic concern because of the warts, but it's also been associated with cervical cancer in the long run," he said, slowly and clearly.

Jolie's mind raced. This was so explicit, so real. Mike had a real sexual disease! She didn't know what to think, or do, how to respond.

"So that's why I wanted to tell you, so that if you decided to become intimate with me, you can make an educated decision."

He looked so sad that Jolie felt a sudden, motherly, Florence Nightingale type of love for him.

"Ever since I found out I had it over a year ago, I've felt awful. I didn't think anybody would ever touch me again." Mike's voice was breaking.

Jolie didn't say anything as she put her hand over his. Perhaps it was sympathy, but that night, when he held her in his arms on the sofa, she sat down in his lap and slowly removed her clothes. She tugged at his pants and undergarments as he looked at her with a grateful kind of disbelief. They slept together, and Mike was so loving, appreciative, and attentive that Jolie felt genuinely in love. She had made the right decision. He was the one, her soul mate, her future husband. When he asked her to move in with him, she eagerly gathered and boxed her belongings. Yoyi and Angel helped her move boxes into the taxi and her new home.

That was twelve months ago. They had been living together all this time, with Jolie expecting that Mike would one day be her husband because she had sacrificed so much for him. She thought about him all day, put much effort into cooking perfect little dinners of his favorite dishes, and even learned to make all sorts of cakes and desserts that he liked in a little mini oven she saved a month's salary to buy. Worst of all, she now had this virus, this sexually transmitted HPV thing that would render her untouchable for Taiwanese men. She checked herself obsessively for warts or bumps, read the same articles on the internet about HPV/genital warts, or in Chinese, *chai hua*, vegetable flowers, and routinely scared herself into near hyperventilation by looking at photographs of the poster boys and girls of HPV: an uncircumcised penis spiked with a crown of genital wart lesions, a vagina that looked rotten and moldy and plain chewed-up. In some pictures, the affected bits were spotted with white mold-like substances in addition to huge areas covered with dirty-looking, flesh-colored, long bubbles in clusters and colonies pushing against one another. Some lesions stood out like the large, flat mushrooms on tree trunks in subtropical forests. In many cases, the parts looked like they were going to fall off.

This was why Jolie was so angry when Mike did nothing to reassure her that he was going to marry her. For the first time, it dawned on her that maybe he never had that intention; he just wanted to know that someone would "touch him" again, and she was his first victim. Who would want her now? Even if she had no warts, she had to tell every future partner about the HPV, because otherwise they would be a hundred times angrier if she slept with them and they grew warts. Maybe in America someone could get away with it, but there are too many virgins in Taiwan for her to get away with something like this. Not to mention she could not lie to someone like that—it would be immoral.

The days passed, and Jolie became more anxious and resentful, but she still waited and hoped. She inspired herself with the traditional Chinese ideal that, with time and effort, one could move someone into reciprocating one's love, if one tried hard enough.

Mike got his GRE scores, applied, and heard back from the graduate school of his choice. He was leaving. Jolie hoped all the way to the airport, fantasizing about him presenting her with a ring just as he was about to go through Immigration and Customs. He gave her a long kiss and hug, then entered the doorway guarded by officers clad in intimidating blue-and-white uniforms. The officers eyed him icily, as if they knew. She watched him through the glass wall at Chiang Kai-shek International Airport. He waved as he got in line for Immigration, and waved again when he disappeared from sight. Jolie waved back, and as she did, she broke down. She had thrown two years of her life away for nothing, she had an STD, and surely nobody would ever touch her again.

Two more years passed. Jolie and her friends were having lunch at a Western-style restaurant.

"It's not your fault," Yoyi said to Jolie. "But I definitely think you could have been meaner to him. At least not as nice as you were."

Angel, who was bouncing a toddler on her knee, nodded.

"I treat my husband like shit, and he just comes back for more."

Immersion

A LOT OF regret fills this little jail cell.

Helen, who sits on the floor next to me, averts her eyes and shifts to turn her entire body away from me. Even Helen with her salon-blonde highlights, fancy jewelry, and expensive clothes no longer has anything witty to say now, no more quotes from American self-help authors or any show-off Chinglish terms she picked up from television.

When you think of the typical woman in her late twenties or early thirties locked up in jail for solicitation and for being part of a prostitution ring, you don't think of someone like me. Sure, I'm pretty enough after makeup to get paid for having sex—my measurements are 34B, 24, 34, and my long, black hair shines like a shampoo commercial right after I leave the salon. However, most of the time I have my hair up in a ponytail or bun, wear thick black-framed glasses, and go about my day without a trace of makeup on. That's how people at school remember me, as a graduate student and teaching assistant at a reputable university. In my diurnal life, I am surrounded by sociology textbooks, highlighters, red pens, and piles of unmarked research papers. Most of my colleagues and the students at school would never dream that I would be a sex worker. In fact, they probably think I'm an old maid. But the truth is, a part-time teaching assistant doesn't get paid much, maybe 350 NT, about ten USD an hour. A girl's got to pay rent, buy clothes, eat, and take care of bills. My parents helped pay my undergraduate tuition, and I promised that once I was a graduate student I would take care of myself. I felt bad that they were still worrying about providing for me when they were half retired and running a little stationery store. I used to watch the store after school, and I knew very few people actually came in and bought anything, and when they did, it was something very small, maybe a ten NT eraser or twenty NT pen. My parents needed every meager NT they made.

I thought it was fate that the day I got my first paycheck from my teaching assistantship, I met Helen. Originally, I had been thrilled that I got the tuition waiver and assistantship, and thought I wouldn't have to worry about my finances. Generally, people are happy when they get their first paycheck. They celebrate; they go out and spend a good chunk of it. I, however, got depressed. The check wasn't enough to cover the monthly rent of thirty thousand NT for my tiny Taipei apartment on the eighth floor of a dingy concrete building. I was going to need a roommate or a second job, possibly both.

It just so happened that Helen, whom I did not know yet, was in line in front of me at Everlast Bank. She fanned herself with a thick stack of cash, showing off. I could smell the greasy glue-and-paper smell of the bills from where I stood. They smelled like envy. I thought to myself, mostly to make myself feel better, that maybe she was a clerk at a small business, and her boss sent her out on a bank run. That was the only reason a woman so young would have an entire paper fan of thousand-NT bills. Maybe I was staring at her money too much because she turned around and grinned right at me.

"It was a good week," she said pleasantly.

"Week?" I asked weakly.

This woman made more in one week than I did in one month. And she read my thoughts.

"Payday disappointing?" she asked, nodding in the direction of the check I was holding.

"No kidding. I won't be able to afford food this month. Eating's overrated, anyway."

"Well, you know, I was just reading a book by a famous American author about how you should never think about how you can't afford something, but instead, you should go look for the money to make it happen. You don't have to cut out food; you could just get yourself a bigger paycheck." Helen mimed a bigger, rectangular paycheck with her index fingers.

Who didn't want to make more money? More easily said than done. I said nothing, but mustered up a smile to go with my polite-but-indifferent nod.

"Let's have some afternoon tea after this if you're not busy. My treat. I think my agent, Tan, might be able to hire someone just like you," Helen said.

Agent? Was she a movie star? Movie stars don't receive cash by the bundle like that. Porn? I was intrigued and desperate enough that after depositing my check I actually followed her out, listening to the crisp click-clacking of her high heels against the cement.

Half an hour later, we sat on the top floor of the fancy new Breeze department store. I took a sip of the imported Darjeeling tea from an elegant porcelain cup painted with yellow flowers, so dainty I thought it might break if I set it down on its matching saucer too hard.

As I sipped my tea, Helen suggested I sell myself into prostitution.

Only she didn't call it that.

"We are freelance entertainers. What we do is public relations, in America they call it PR. Prostitutes—hell no! Prostitutes have no control over which clients they take and sex is their only trade. We PR girls often have other talents or professions that we do during the day. You said you are a teacher? I'm pretty sure we have another teacher, too. There are also a few housewives, a law student, and I work at a cosmetics counter a few days a week. I don't do it for the money, though. I do it for the employee discounts and endless free samples."

Helen went on and on, and I listened with my mouth open.

"So what do you think?"

"I'm sorry. I can't do anything like that," I said, and meant it.

What would my parents say if they knew that the college education they paid for only amounted to my becoming a part-time prostitute? I reached for my jacket and purse, but Helen waved over a waiter carrying a tray filled with exquisite desserts: blueberry cheesecake, tiramisu, cream puffs, and green tea mochi. I would have said no, but before I said anything, my stomach growled, not just briefly, but two obnoxious, drawn-out *gwwwoo-ow-ow-ow* sounds. Helen laughed and took two desserts from the waiter's tray and pushed them in front of me. Too embarrassed to object, I picked up a little silver fork and ate.

After tea and dessert, Helen handed me two business cards, one black, one pink. The pink one was hers. ("Call me if you need anything, or just want to have afternoon tea again!") The black one belonged to her agent. ("His name is Tan, tell him I recommended you. He's lovely.") I accepted the cards with every intention of throwing them in the trash as soon as I was out of her sight, but soon forgot them at the bottom of the canvas bag I was carrying that day.

The next month, however, as I was withdrawing cash from an ATM, just about emptying out the savings account I'd been slowly adding to with Chinese New Year red envelopes since I was a little girl, I remembered Helen and her offer. My dad helped set up the account for me when I was in third grade and I was supposed to add to it, not deplete it. There's no harm in having tea with Helen again, I figured. Besides, I am a sociologist looking for material for my research project. Maybe I should look into this industry. There could be thesis material in Helen's underground PR girl ring. If this didn't work out, I'd have to do something gerontology-related, and I didn't feel like spending the next five years of my life in an old people's home.

I went through everything in my closet. I tried on so many dresses and suits, a mountain of clothes and hangers had formed on the floor of my closet by the time I decided on a simple black shirt and jeans.

I arrived early at the top floor of the department store and waited for Helen. I must have read every item and description on the menu five times, though the words slipped through my mind without registering. Finally, my new friend arrived in a slinky white dress with crystals on the neckline and slinky fabric that hugged her body. Her brown sunglasses had very prominent logos on the side, probably an expensive designer brand.

"So, you changed your mind?" Helen's lips sparkled from light pink lipstick with a glimmering sheen.

"I just wanted to find out more," I said, pushing up my glasses and fancying myself a sociologist doing important, undercover fieldwork.

"I talked to Tan about you. He would love to meet you in person. In fact, he said that he might stop by soon," Helen said. "He's bringing the book."

"What book?" I was taken aback by her springing Tan on me, but at the same time intrigued. After all, this was what I was here for, wasn't it?

"It's the book with all the girls. A catalog. It lists everybody's measurements, includes a current salon picture, and also specifies interests, hobbies, talents, and sexual preferences." Helen gestured with her hands as she spoke, like it was the most normal thing in the world, a menu of purchasable woman.

"Sexual . . . preferences? You mean like if I prefer a man or a woman?" I asked.

"That, of course, is a basic thing, telling us what you are open to. But also, do you like S&M? Are you good at role playing? Are you dominant or submissive? Are you willing to dress in costumes such as schoolgirl outfits? Do you like rubber garments, pain, or bondage? What about feet or other fetishes?"

I knew such things existed, but I never thought about them in conjunction with myself, or regular people. Were all the clients perverts? I'd only had groping-beneath-covers sex with an ex-boyfriend from college, and it had been a while. Had all men become perverts while I was busy studying?

Tan arrived a few minutes later, dressed in a cream-colored suit that contrasted with his brown sunglasses. His brown briefcase, which he set on the table after shaking my hand, sported a heavy-looking metal lock. I wondered if the briefcase was filled with cash or shiny gold bars, like in the gangster movies.

"You have a real air of purity about you," Tan said, looking me up and down.

He unlocked the briefcase and took out a leather-covered book, one like the typical salon-quality photo album. It featured women in schoolgirl outfits or white dresses, with innocent, wide-eyed facial expressions; whip-wielding women in rubber suits with blood-red temptress lips; women with bleached hair in bikinis; punk rock chicks on motorcycles. The text beneath the pictures was too small for me to read quickly, but I noticed numbers in bold: height, weight, and the bust-waist-hip measurements of each of the women. My mind raced as I pictured borrowing Tan's catalogue and quoting parts of it for my master's thesis. It might even be published as a book. Of course it would be published as a book. Sex sells, after all. Maybe I should interview the women and get some fascinating, in-depth case studies.

"I think you would be great as a sexy librarian," Tan said, interrupting my thoughts. "And you are very educated. You will be able to carry on a good conversation, which high-level businessmen and government officials love."

"Government officials?" I asked.

"Sure, we have all types of clients. Many rich and influential men, and they are rather selective. I only sign the best girls, classy women like the two of you. And, of course, utmost secrecy among all parties is imperative. We don't PR and tell here."

"So what would I have to do?" I asked, already plotting to avoid legal issues by drafting disclaimers, getting releases signed, and using pseudonyms in my thesis.

"Spend some time with the men. You can pick and choose which clients and appointments you want to take, and spend some quality time with them at an exclusive location."

The exclusive locations turned out to be seedy motels on the outskirts of Taipei. Between gray walls and faded wallpaper, I learned to say the things each client wanted to hear, act out the parts they expected of me while wearing the outfits that made their dicks hard. I became one of Tan's best PR girls because I took such great notes. Back home on my laptop, I had an Excel file that listed information about each client. The whole time I had my thesis on my mind. Nobody had done research like mine before in Taiwan—it was groundbreaking fieldwork—no sociologist in the past had made such sacrifices for her work, personally *xia hai*, waded into the murky sex-worker ocean, as it were. I could become a famous author and be invited to appear on TV shows, maybe even have my own call-in talk show. That would be in addition to traveling all over Taiwan on speaking engagements and university lectures with my bestselling book, of course.

In short, the work sucked me in. Every other day, I spent a few hours of my free time in a motel with one man or another. They gave me gifts: spa memberships, designer bags, jewelry, and of course, cash. I documented everything in my Excel file, meticulously recording each non-monetary gift and its market value.

Up until the day the police barged into the motel room and arrested me for one account of solicitation and a second of adultery, adultery still being illegal according to Taiwanese law, on a certain level, I really believed I was only doing serious sociological research.

"It's called immersion," I said to the police officer, a young man with a crew cut and pockmarked cheeks.

"I don't care what you call it, doll. It's illegal."

"I am a graduate student in sociology. It's a sociological term, to immerse yourself in the environment of the people or careers you are studying. I'm not doing anything wrong. It's research for my thesis."

He made me stick my hands out in front of me and handcuffed my wrists.

What happened was one girl was caught by the wife of one client, and the police got involved. That PR girl made a deal with the police and gave up Tan's information, which led to a search warrant and arrest. Naturally, the police got all the phone numbers, the detailed menu of girls in Tan's book, and all the evidence they needed to catch most, if not all, of us.

"A total of nineteen girls were caught," Helen whispered.

"No men?"

"Who cares about the Johns?"

"What about Tan?"

"He was booked for possession of all sorts of illegal drugs, I heard. Amphetamines, ketamine, cocaine, and ecstasy. He'll be in jail for much longer than all of us put together, or maybe they'll just put him in a chair and *buzzzzzz*."

I shuddered.

Some women would be bailed out by their (very angry, probably ready-for-divorce) husbands, and some by friends or siblings, but who would bail me out? I couldn't ask my colleagues. I would be fired from my teaching assistantship, dismissed by my university, which despite accepting students of all religions, identified itself as a conservative Catholic institution. A PR girl for a TA wouldn't do.

"Do you think one of our clients would bail us out?" I asked Helen.

Helen threw her head back, laughing like a crazy person. "You think those men would touch us with a ten-foot pole right now? They will deny everything and anything! Those men don't want to be associated with prostitutes! It would ruin their careers, businesses, marriages . . . are you nuts?"

Helen had never called herself or me a prostitute before.

I really don't want to call my parents. I can just see it—Chinese New Year, everybody in the family whispering about my scandalous lifestyle, how my parents failed to bring me up right, how I used to be such a good girl but see how I am ruined now, how nobody will ever marry me, a tainted, worn-out shoe . . .

Cat Spring Roll

Tina never liked cats. Her mother always said they were *yin*, dark, connected to spirits and the underworld, possibly evil. Tina hadn't known that Bo had a cat. If she had, she would never have agreed to go on a date with him in the first place, would not have passively gone to dinners, lunches, movies with him for two months, and consented, mostly out of wanting to end the boredom of his courtship, to become engaged and married soon afterward.

Tina had been to Bo's house a few times and liked what she saw: a garage large enough for two cars at the entrance, a large living room, a narrow hallway opening on the left to a cozy master bedroom, on the right a beige-tiled kitchen and bath, ending in a sun-facing back room for laundry. The modest furniture, Taiwanese and traditional, combined just the right amount of red wood, leather, and glass. Marbled white tile covered the floors, and the walls were painted the white-yellow color of rice.

They were already engaged by the time she saw the cat, unfortunately. When the cat emerged, Bo picked up the animal and rubbed his face in its fur, startling Tina with this uncharacteristic display of intimacy. The ratty tabby looked at her, opened its jaw in a silent meow, leaped out of her fiancé's arms and trotted into the bedroom, tail fluffed up and erect. Tina noticed that the bedroom had no door. In fact, except for the bathroom, all the rooms were doorless. How strange. Maybe it was a *feng shui* thing, to get rid of fighting doors or something. Maybe Bo had them taken out, or the house came like that.

They married in a hurry because men were not supposed to marry in their twenty-ninth year; it's very bad luck according to Chinese fortunetelling. All the arrangements felt rushed—Tina hardly got to enjoy being a bride. The ceremony itself was simple, merely involving the signing of documents in the presence of two witnesses. The wedding banquet followed. The banquet, usually a high point of Chinese weddings, seemed no grander an occasion than a large family meal at a restaurant, in this case.

"You are marrying into a good family," Mrs. Yeh, Tina's new mother-in-law, said. "You will see that our wealth lies in the fact that we do not show it off in lavish wedding ceremonies and fancy banquets. We know better than that. One thing I can assure you is that you will never starve."

Tina never assumed that she would starve, single or married. She did wonder, however, about the honeymoon she felt she had been tricked out of. Bo had promised Tina a trip to Hawaii as soon as the busy season at the television station was done, but she wasn't holding her breath.

Tina did not know if she loved Bo, but he seemed a suitable match for her. Stability was a good thing; plus she had long since tired of meeting the awkward men her parents set her up with.

Bo and Tina did not consummate their marriage on their wedding night. Bo, a deadline looming over his head, went back to his office to edit clips. Tina spent most of the evening taking off her makeup and getting situated in her new home. She unpacked, organized and reorganized closets and drawers, and finally dozed off on the living room sofa as one late-night variety show blended into the next.

When Bo came home, his bride was already in bed. She pretended to be asleep, and he didn't try to wake her.

At three in the morning, the tabby came into the bedroom, howling. The ugly cat noises woke Tina with a start. She opened her eyes to see the fat ochre-and-black cat land on her husband's chest. The cat crouched on Bo's chest in a way that made Tina think it was going to attack her, and she nearly fell out of bed trying to dodge its claws when it pounced on a spot right next to Tina. The cat dug its claws into the blanket—foggy yellow eyes strange in the moonlight shining through a high window. The cat hissed at Tina and let out a loud meow which turned into a howl. Bo woke.

"Hello, Baby." His left hand reached behind the cat's ugly little head, scratching gently.

The cat's howl turned to a persistent whine. It spun around and sprawled lengthwise across Bo's chest so that the claws of its hind leg scraped Tina's elbow. She sat up on her side of the bed, terribly bothered. Bo and the furball's eyes were closed, but the cat's throat jangled every few seconds, answered by a humming sound from the sleeping man. The two of them obviously always slept like this, humming and purring, a combination of sounds more irritating than anything Tina had ever heard, at least at this time of night.

The man-and-cat noises irked her so much she moved to the couch like an evicted spouse, post-quarrel. This was a bad beginning to their married life, and she knew it.

Three weeks later, both Mr. and Mrs. Yeh had deep, green-and-brown tired marks under their eyes. Bo's were from few hours of sleep and the stress of work, Tina's from being awakened by the cat every night. From any other person's point of view, being woken up by a cat at three in the morning wasn't a big deal, but Tina was so incensed by the disturbance that she instantly turned into an insomniac. She would spend three to five in the morning watching television or reading a romance novel in the living room under a fluorescent light, which would make her still more awake and irritated. Finally, she would pass out on the couch, and her husband, up at seven and leaving the house at around seven twenty, would peck her on the cheek on his way out. The cat, eager to please, always followed him to the glass doors and saw him off with round eyes.

"Bye, Baby." He said this with great tenderness before opening the electronic garage door and going to his car.

Tina suspected his beloved *Baby* was the cat, not her. Through sleepy eyes, she watched the metal garage door curl up like a sleeping bag to the ceiling, then lower itself slowly after her husband's green Honda backed away. A small, black remote controlled the door. Tina had one, too, and sometimes she played with it. It struck her as odd that there were barely any doors in the apartment, but in order to leave one had to open this incredibly heavy garage door which even Superman couldn't lift unless he had the remote control. The grooved metal curled up and down, *clink clink whoo whoo*, like a strange creature's metamorphosis being recorded and fast forwarded on the Nature Channel.

Tina worked off and on taking cases from an East Asian translation agency in Taipei. During the day, she sat in front of her laptop with her multiple Japanese-Chinese dictionaries, alternating between typing, watching TV, snacking, and dozing off. She wanted to punish the cat for ruining her sleep every night and hogging her husband, but the animal hid from her in the daytime, only to emerge, purring or howling noisily, when he came home.

Upon entering the living room, Bo sat down on the sofa and took the cat instead of Tina into his lap and arms. Peeved, Tina clanked woks and pans and chopsticks against bowls, making as much noise as possible in the kitchen, but Bo never seemed to notice.

Every night the cat came in. Tina developed an irrational hatred for the animal, yet she was afraid of it because it was so *yin*, its impure yellow eyes glinting in the dark, and because it had sharp claws. She had seen the streaks—long, red marks on her husband, which he said the cat just made inadvertently. Tina could imagine what it would look like if the tabby really wanted to kill someone; she pictured her own stomach sliced open by a few cat slashes, the bowels pouring out like bloody noodle soup. Her fear only fed her hatred, and sometimes, when she was startled out of sleep by a sudden "MEEOOOW!" she temporarily forgot she was a civilized human being and hissed at the cat.

Her husband only ran his hand along the cat's spine with a sleepy smile on his face and hummed. The cat purred, and the louder it purred, the more it seemed to be saying to Tina, "He's mine, he's mine. He likes me, not you."

Sunday morning, Tina awoke with a craving for freshly steamed crab with sweet orange eggs beneath the shell. She could still hear Bo's snoring when she got dressed to go to the morning market.

"Damn, where's the remote?" Tina muttered out loud.

She searched the garage and living room, leaving the glass door wide open though she knew she wasn't supposed to, since there was no screen door and mosquitoes were always getting in. Finally, she found the device wedged between two sofa cushions. She must have accidentally pushed it in there last night in her sleep. Locking the glass door with her left hand, she pressed the remote with her right. The metal door curled up in slow motion. Impatient, she ducked under the metal spring roll as soon as there was enough space for her to do so. Tina left the garage door half curled up so she didn't have to wait for it again when she returned with a cart full of groceries.

The morning market cheered Tina up. She loved the fresh fruit, live seafood still smelling of the ocean, moist vegetables picked just hours ago from the hills. The liveliness of a bustling market always appealed to her more than the sterile supermarkets with fluorescent lights and refrigerated, sagging fruit. In the morning market, farmers hawked their selection of fresh ingredients, cut samples for customers to taste ("See how sweet, this watermelon!"), butchers slammed cleavers down on wooden cutting boards, and old people shook their heads, haggling over a few NT even as they accepted pink-white plastic bags filled with their selections from vendors.

Tina would make a fantastic meal today. She hadn't given up on her marriage yet, and a delicious meal might be just the thing to fix her relationship with her husband. In her cart sat snow apples, crab wrapped in newspaper, vegetables, half of a large salmon knotted in a plastic bag, seasoned pig ears, and stringy tofu. Tina walked home with her heart and cart brimming.

It was already bright out, so Tina wanted to open the garage door all the way to allow some sun into the apartment, something she usually did during the daytime. She fumbled in her pockets for the black remote and pressed the green button that said "up". The door dutifully curled upwards, but as it clink-clanked upwards, Tina heard the horrible howling and squeal of a cat—her husband's cat. There was the sound of claws scratching against metal and all the time howls, horrible intestine-twisting howls, the kind of noise one imagined permeated the deepest levels of Buddhist hell.

Hands quivering, Tina stopped the garage door and pressed the "down" button. As the door uncurled itself, a bloody, furry mass landed with a soft plop inside the garage, a few feet from Tina. Her husband's Baby, his precious daughter, the ugly yellow-eyed tabby was writhing in blood, fur, and exposed flesh on the ground. All its legs seemed to be broken, chewed up then spewed out by the carnivorous garage door. Tina left her groceries in front of her home and rushed down the street in horror. She felt the accusing, unclean yellow eyes of the cat following her all the way.

Rainy Night Stand-Up

IT WAS THE first time Lena was going to have unprotected sex in her life. No condoms cluttered her or her husband's backpacks, and she was officially off birth control. After all, they were not getting any younger, and Jon had been pestering her about having a baby ever since they got married.

Three hours ago, they got off the Jing Shan 611 bus and walked down a small path in the drizzling rain. Their destination? A big sign that read "Golden Springs," which Lena thought sounded vaguely like a euphemism for something dirty, though she wasn't sure what. The place was scenic enough: each unit was a little wooden hut with an enclosed yard containing a large hot tub lined with tile and surrounded with wooden planks. If it were not for the chill of the steady rain, this would be the ideal romantic celebration of their one-year anniversary. Soon after their arrival, the rain started coming down harder, violently bouncing off the surface of the hot spring water. Swirls of steam rose from the pool, which smelled faintly of sulfur and hardboiled eggs.

"It's too bad it's raining so hard." Lena peeled off her wet jeans in a decidedly unsexy manner, yanking her wet feet out of the last bit of pant leg, and shivered herself into a terrycloth bathrobe. She had prepared lingerie, but it was too cold for that, and as far as she was concerned, too cold for sex.

"We can get in the hot spring later. Maybe the rain will die down," Jon said, although he seemed visibly disappointed that Lena was hiding her body in a gigantic garment made out of towel material instead of something lacy or see-through. After all, he was the one who had bought her the lingerie, so he knew exactly what he hoped, if not expected, to see on her.

He changed into his pajamas and got in bed beside Lena, who had already ducked under the covers and rested her head sideways on a pillow. Jon turned on the television and flicked through a series of channels: the Taiwanese eight o'clock news, Star Movies, an infomercial, finally settling on stand-up comedy on HBO.

A burst of laughter from Jon woke Lena up. Through a sleepy haze, she heard the comedian's words.

"My five-year-old daughter has nothing important to say. Never. When you're five years old, trust me, you have nothing important to say. I just tell her to zip it."

Lena felt disturbed by the man's dismissiveness.

"And people, if you have a choice, have boys. Boys just break a few things, no big deal. Girls—girls are a whole other matter. Girls are evil. They are manipulative, devious, and they will worm their way inside your head and drive you crazy. My five-year-old daughter, God bless her soul, is the devil incarnate."

Lena could not believe that Jon, sitting beside her, was chuckling at this gender-stereotyping, sexist joke. She was wide awake now.

"Not only are girls and boys different, men and women are different. A woman can stop having sex or lose interest in it any time. She's distracted by something, and she kicks you out of bed. A guy, however, needs to finish. He can't just stop and push the 'off' button on sex. He has no control. If I was having sex with a hot young woman, and she turned around and bashed my mom's head in, I would think, *that's messed up,* but I would continue fucking her—"

Lena wondered if the comedian's mother was watching this.

"My wife and I don't have sex anymore. But I still enjoy looking at her, even if she hates being looked at now. She is beautiful, a real woman. You know those twenty-two-year-old girls who walk around with lollipops and high heels and ponytails and *talk like, like this, you know, like, yeah*? Those are not women. Those are *girls.* Girls have tits. Women, real women like my wife, have dangly breasts and long, chewed-up nipples. Now that's a woman. A girl does not become a woman until she's had some people come out of her vagina, ruin her body, and trample every single last one of her dreams."

Jon laughed uproariously. Lena sat up.

"You actually think that is funny?" she asked, fuming.

Jon looked surprised. "Well, yes, I mean it's exaggerated, but there's an element of truth in it that makes it funny." Jon shrugged.

"You think a woman's body being ruined and her dreams trampled over because of getting married and having kids is funny? Chewed-up nipples are funny?" Lena asked.

"In the context, it was funny, but of course I wouldn't actually laugh at a woman's body in real life."

"Then why would you laugh at the joke? There's nothing funny about it. It's completely disrespectful and insulting toward women. His wife had kids for him, fed their kids from her breasts, and now he's laughing at her body."

"It's just a joke."

"Do you think it would be a joke if I got stretch marks and messed-up breasts and had my dreams shattered by our future children? Would you laugh at me?"

"Of course not."

"What about the stuff he said about kids, not listening to what kids say just because they are five? What if the child was hurt or molested? If we have a kid, will you not listen to her either? Because you thought that joke was funny, too," Lena said. "And do you also think that little girls are evil and conniving?"

"No," Jon said, stiffening. "That's not fair."

"Because if you are even a little bit like that comedian, then I don't want to have a child with you," Lena said, pulling her bathrobe tighter around her waist beneath the covers.

"Don't you think that you're overreacting?" Jon let out a dismissive little laugh. "Are you seriously saying that you don't want to have kids with me just because I laughed at a stupid joke? Doesn't that seem excessive?"

"It depends on the joke. Something small like that can be an indication of who you are and what kind of parent and husband you will be, and how you will treat your child and your wife in the future. As a woman, I already have enough trouble worrying that, if we one day have kids, when they are teenagers and I am middle-aged you might run away with a hot little twenty-two-year-old. Now I also have to worry about you laughing at my body, and also how you might treat our daughter if we have one?"

Lena's tears spilled down her cheeks. A spark of lightning lit up the skies outside, visible through the glass doors separating the hot tub from their room.

"I already said that I would never laugh at your body," Jon muttered.

Lena continued to sob, clawing blindly through her tears at a Kleenex box on the nightstand.

"In fact, if anything, I feel offended that you think I would be like that. You should have more faith and trust in me. I am your husband and you should know me better than that."

Lena crumpled a wet Kleenex and tossed it in the direction of a wicker wastebasket, where it joined a small mound of Kleenex snowballs that had missed their mark.

"Regardless," she sniffed, "of all the shows in the world, you happen to watch this stupid, misogynistic stand-up comedy, right before we were planning to have unprotected sex for the first time? What are the odds of that? We watch TV together all the time, and nothing like this has ever happened before. I think this means something."

"Well, if it's not this, it's some other thing. I don't think you really want to have kids. You are looking for an excuse," Jon said, getting out of bed.

"I was totally willing to try to get pregnant, you know that," Lena protested. "I'm not on birth control anymore, and I brought the lingerie—"

"Willing to? I want you to *want* a child, not just say you are willing to, like I'm forcing you. Do you want a child or do you not? If you never want a child, then I think we should go our separate ways and not waste any more of each other's time."

"Are you threatening to divorce me if I don't have a kid with you?" Lena's voice was inflected and incredulous. "Are you living in biblical times, classical China or something? Get rid of your wife because she doesn't give you kids? I thought we loved each other. You can't really love me that much if you want a divorce just because I'm not giving you a kid after *one* year of marriage! Do you realize how horrible and crazy you sound?"

"You're the one who suddenly doesn't want a kid because of a stand-up comic's joke on television."

"We've only been married for one year! If anybody else was married for one year and her husband was pressuring her to have kids, I would tell her that's really fast, probably too soon. I'm trying my best to be a good sport, and I came here with the full intention of trying to have a baby because you were so eager. But now, maybe not. Especially if you're threatening divorce. Why would I commit to you or to having a child with you if you so easily demand a breakup?" Lena, hysterical with tears, practically huffed the moist balls of Kleenex she held up to her face.

"I thought we were in love," she continued. "I have never thought about divorce, ever, and I can't believe you are saying things like this."

Jon shook his head as if he thought his wife was insane and sat back down on the bed. Lena threw back the covers and moved toward the glass doors.

"You're overreacting," Jon said. "Come back to bed. Look, the resort provides free condoms. We can use a condom if you want."

Lena ignored him and opened the glass door to the patio. She walked into the rain, which landed like frozen needles on her bare hands and face. She put one foot into the hot tub, then another, and slowly removed her bathrobe, letting it fall into the water. She stood naked in the rain, in the steam rising from the water's surface. She breathed in the mineral scent of sulfur, which brought to her mind the image of golden mountains and cliffs, the source of the spring water. Something clicked inside her, and with that vision, just like that, she knew she could let go. She did not need Jon anymore, nor did she want him. She wanted the mountains, not this prison on earth.

Jon watched her through the glass door. Lena looked away from him and sat down, submerging her body in the water. The heat soothed her legs, back, and shoulders. All her worries—Jon's desire for a baby, the prospect of her juggling her one and a half jobs and a pregnancy and baby—dissolved.

She had thought that a child was her next step in life. Now she saw what the real step had to be: leaving. The house and mortgage were under his name, so she would not be burdened. She had her job, she had a decent body not yet "ruined" by childbirth, nipples perfectly tiny and pink, and she intended to keep them that way until she found a man who was worthy.

Passport Baby

WHEN MY HUGELY pregnant balloon of a wife and I got on a plane to the United States, we had one goal: to have an American baby. The timing was impeccably planned to fit into the visit allowed by our costly three-month tourist visas. Our prize: Seng Seng, my nervous, large-headed son; the bruise marks that my wife, in labor, squeezed onto my wrist; and special front row seats on the airplane behind the galleys so we could use a bassinet attached to the wall. Blonde stewardesses cooed at our baby all the way from San Francisco to Taipei. And the final reward: when Seng Seng turns twenty-one, he will apply to his government to bring us all to America.

At least that's the plan. My wife's plan, mostly.

Here's another new plan of hers: hiring help at home.

The new maid, Lin Lin, could be anywhere between nineteen and twenty-six—you can't tell with the baby-faced ones. She's pretty enough, I guess, with soft Southeast Asian features similar to many Taiwanese women, but with paler, porcelain-like skin. When she wears her hair in a ponytail, I almost mistake her for my wife sometimes, except for her slim figure in contrast with my wife's generous, post-pregnant form.

I don't think about either of them in a lustful way. At this point women are a tiring presence in my life: three of them, all under my roof. The scariest one of them all? My mother-in-law.

"Why don't you let me buy you a new suit, you're always dressed so shabbily. You're a businessman. Appearances are important," my mother-in-law says, not even looking at me but checking her professionally manicured nails.

"This suit was very expensive," I say. It's true.

"But it's old! An expensive old suit is much worse than a cheap suit. It's shabby to wear old clothes. At least put on one of those new shirts I got you."

"That's not necessary."

"You think nothing is necessary. Just put one on, they weren't expensive, two for a thousand NT, marked down at the department store sale."

"I tried one on a few days ago, remember? It made me itch." It's an allergy I inherited from my mother's side of the family. Synthetic fabric leads to my breaking out in hives every time.

"You're just neurotic, imagining things. You're not a real man. My daughter married a fake."

In addition to having an unreasonable personality, my mother-in-law also has diabetes. No doubt her kidneys will worsen and require dialysis every three weeks, emptying our bank accounts while her bitterness eats up our souls.

One night, I was reading the evening paper in the living room, minding my own business, and in she walked wearing her favorite green nightgown. She gave me the full-frontal view of her sagging, scary body veiled in the color of moldy, spotted olives. I don't even remember the question she asked me, so stunned and scarred was my mind. She had the longest nipples I had ever seen, long, droopy ones like a stack of one-NT coins with dark areoles at the base of each sag, so dark one could see their shadows through an entire layer of fabric.

Her daughter's nipples aren't especially small or short either. I'm glad she keeps her bra on most of the time. It's too much, really, the sight of bare breasts, so real with swollen, uneven, goose-bumpy areolae, especially after the baby when the veins showed like tree branches and the orbs were engorged with fresh human milk, nipples inflated into balls. Luckily, my loving wife finds the fact that I like her underwear to be kinky. She imagines I have a brassiere fetish. She does not know what horror I feel every time she pops a breast out of her convenience bra, ripe melon from a sack, to feed Seng Seng.

My wife is attractive enough. Just not to me, not in that way anymore.

Something happened to my overgrown schoolgirl. Once she was adorable, the smile on her peach-like face or a glimpse of a smooth limb always stirring something I thought was happiness in my heart. Even the way she bit into a steamed bun I used to find moving.

Now, watching her eat just frightens me.

When we were dating, she only let me hold her and touch her through a bra and panties or one-piece swimming suit. The transition point was our wedding night: after the ceremony with its toasts and drinks and clothes-changing and bowing, she climbed on top of me and rather forcefully claimed me as her husband. Perhaps it was the stress of the wedding, the champagne, shock, or fear in response to her aggressiveness, but I could barely get it up for my bride.

Now, she won't leave me alone. Sometimes she reaches for me in front of her mother; it's indecent, all those ideas the Chinese version of *Cosmopolitan* must be putting in her head. She buys imported lace nighties from France and Italy, and a ridiculous assortment of candles and massage oils with dirty-sounding names. Half the time, I want to run away. The rest of the time, I just want to watch television or sleep.

I don't want to be like one of those tormented men on TV who are always being nagged by insatiable wives. I've considered stocking up on the little blue pills that one can buy whispering, leaning over the counter, from most Taiwanese drugstores. Not that I've ever done it. I'm only thirty-one; I'd have to be at least thirty-five to stoop that low.

From the outside, our middle-class home looks modest. My wife and her mother picked everything they wanted from various home décor catalogues and traditional furniture stores. I appreciate that nothing matches. In the living room, a sofa of crocodile skin and a floral-patterned love seat cluster around a modern, wavy-looking coffee table, the TV an enormous fifty-inch thing balanced on a small brass table with S-shaped legs. Ratty tapestries depicting mythological menageries hang side by side with framed Chinese watercolors on our light green and cream-colored walls. Curtains line every window and doorway: heavy cotton in the living room, lace in the bedrooms, translucent plastic—sticky from old grease—in the kitchen. The kitchen, unlike most Taiwanese ones, boasts a built-in oven and the two-door, ice-making refrigerator my wife said she always wanted. A row of appliances lines the marble counter: automatic can opener, four-slice toaster, ten-cup coffee maker, blender, food processor. Too bad all those wonderful chef's aids haven't produced as many satisfying meals as one might hope.

I'm proud to own a house in the best neighborhood in Shing Tien while most of Taipei squats in tiny apartments. But this house has its flaws. Soundproofing was an issue I never considered before. How could I? I didn't know my bride was going to be a screamer. And when she makes too much noise, I lose my erection. The idea of her mother hearing us might just drive me into celibacy.

It's a good thing that first the pregnancy, and now the baby, keeps my wife preoccupied. We must be doing something wrong, however, because my son is a fussy bundle of nerves. Any sound at all startles him horribly, and after a few such shocks he wails. A dog bark, a door slam, or a car siren going off in the neighborhood—anything can set him off.

"You're me, Seng Seng. You're nervous and feel threatened by the women around you. I agree. They're scary," I whisper to him.

He looks at me with large, watery eyes. He wants me to stop talking, I can tell. *Shut up, useless dad.* I shake my head, folding my fingers around one of his chubby feet, and sure enough, he bursts into tears.

Aside from his mother's sizeable nipples, Lin Lin is the only remedy to Seng Seng's tantrums. The maid loves it when Seng Seng goes off; it gives her an excuse to drop whatever housework she is doing and run to take care of the baby. She can hold him for hours, watching television, napping with him, singing him Vietnamese songs. For all I know those songs might be a bad influence on him, but what can I do—the child likes her. She likes to grab Seng Seng and swing him around, something that makes me nervous because I think his arms will be dislocated from the rest of his body at the armpits.

My wife's jealousy flares when she sees that the child she carried for nine months in her womb prefers Lin Lin instead. She yells at Lin Lin for trivial things such as a dirty corner in the bathroom or an unscrubbed bathtub, though her anger never lasts long. After all, the maid makes it possible for her to take naps in the middle of the day. I tried to get a raise for Lin Lin for her extra work with the baby, but my wife, who manages household finances, refused.

"She does not deserve it. The baby is only an excuse for her to avoid housework. Besides, who changes his diapers? Who gives him baths and gets wet when he kicks or pees everywhere? Who feeds him and gets vomited all over when he's sick? Me! And you want to give the maid more money?"

Even when Seng Seng is being difficult and we are exhausted, neither of us approaches my mother-in-law for help because she acts like we're abusing her or treating her like help when we ask her to do the tiniest baby-favor for us. You would think that a grandmother wouldn't mind taking her grandson out in his stroller after dinner, but she screws up her face when we ask.

"You think I'm old and useless and have nothing better to do than your chores? Young people these days, no sense of responsibility. Old Mrs. Jian's children would never ask her to lift a finger to do housework for them. When are you going to begin to treat me right, huh?"

She wasn't a good mother; how could she suddenly become a good grandmother? her daughter mutters under her breath.

This morning, I woke up to a disconcerting silence in the house. Something was wrong. I could feel it in my bones. We had slept too long, too well. Sitting up in bed, I spotted the empty crib at the foot of our bed. I shook my wife, who was curled up to my left, hogging the extra blanket that she had rolled into a big sausage-like thing sandwiched between her legs.

"Where is Seng Seng?"

"Huh?" She let go of the sausage and rubbed her eyes.

"Seng Seng isn't in his bed."

"Maybe Lin Lin took him."

I didn't like the idea of Lin Lin "taking" the baby. I shoved my feet into plastic house slippers, almost tripping on them, and pushed open the bedroom door. The living room was empty. Someone had left the TV on last night, mute, flickering. Dust flew uncannily in rays of sunlight peeking through unevenly drawn curtains.

I knocked on the maid's door, then, met with no answer, banged.

"Open up, Lin Lin, is Seng Seng in there?"

I opened the door with more force than necessary, thinking it would be locked from the inside. Lin Lin's room was messy and impersonal: the bed unmade, towels lying around, the trashcan overflowing, but there were no photos or underwear or anything that indicated even the gender of its resident.

I headed for my study, next to Lin Lin's room, and reached into the secret panel in the top right drawer, which yielded some objects. There used to be a few thousand NT in the drawer since we were going to pay the cable company and gas people—that was gone. My IDs and bankbooks were there, but where was my wife's ID? And Seng Seng's American passport and birth certificate?

I felt sick as I remembered that we had no identification of any sort from Lin Lin because she wasn't legally hired. All we knew was her name, which could have been fake. She might not even be Vietnamese. She could be Thai, Filipino, Malaysian, even Taiwanese—there was no way for us to know. How would we find her, and our son, the American?

Mine

SERENA LIFTED UP her favorite sweater, which bore on its left, where the heart would have been, a pink wound. She reached deep into the washing machine and fished out the culprit, her husband's red washcloth, and threw it against the wall, where it splattered and then fell to the tiled floor, immediately creating a puddle.

Serena sat down on the cold tile floor, tears streaming down her cheeks. It wasn't just the sweater and washcloth—it was his affair. The ruined sweater was a glaring symbol of his excessive overtime at the hospital, the mysterious late-night calls, and his overall lack of interest in her. She sensed something was going on, and for months she had been waiting for him to slip up, to break down out of guilt and confess, to come home with the clichéd lipstick-on-the-collar. But he was discreet, and she too prideful to breathe a word.

Her parents had brought her up like a princess, and princesses lived happily ever after, didn't they? As a young girl, she went to a private music school, played the piano and flute, wore pretty dresses and jewelry made of 24k gold and real diamonds. Her petite bourgeoisie Taiwanese family groomed her to become the perfect trophy wife. Many eligible bachelors and their families were interested in Serena, a plump-cheeked, curly-haired musician who looked like a porcelain doll. She could have become Mrs. Ding, daughter-in-law of Powers Media Group, or Mrs. May, future owner of the pharmaceutical empire, Bioway. Ultimately she chose Mike Sei, a young doctor interning at Fu Da Hospital. She gave him her sweetest, dimpled smile on their first date because she knew her parents liked him the best.

The wedding banquet was an explosion of red, an elaborate twelve-course meal. Only the best champagne and XO reddened the cheeks of over two hundred guests all evening. Serena, in true princess fashion, changed outfits five times, since traditionally, the wedding banquet was a fashion show for a Taiwanese bride. Entire gown rental businesses depended on this tradition for business revenue. Serena got the fanciest gown package. Her first dress was an ethereal, Western-style ball gown with white feathers and Swarovski crystals. Next in line was a sultry, purple silk dress that showed off her curves, followed by a pink cocktail dress, and a gold gown covered with dazzling sequins. The bridal secretary, an expert beautician and MAC makeup artist, tamed her curls and did her makeup differently with each change of outfit. The finale was a traditional red Chinese *qipao*. It was so tight Serena could hardly breathe while she stood at the exit handing out red wedding sweets to departing guests.

But she was happy because she saw how happy her parents were. She'd watched their faces all night, and there was something more than joy in their faces. Something resembling relief, as if a weight had been lifted off their shoulders because their little girl was going to live happily ever after and they could stop worrying.

The phone rang, interrupting Serena's fond recollection of her banquet.

"Is Mrs. Sei there?" a woman asked.

"This is she. Who's calling?"

"I am your husband's girlfriend."

For a few seconds, Serena forgot to breathe.

"I have a business proposal for you," the woman continued.

"Excuse me?" Serena considered hanging up the phone, but the woman continued talking.

"Five million NT. Tax-free. You can live on the interest alone for the rest of your life, or buy yourself a nice apartment. If you divorce your husband, the money is all yours," the woman said in a business-like tone filled with confidence.

"Are you crazy? Who are you? You can't just call people's houses like this, I have no idea who you are. You have the wrong number. I'm going to hang up—"

"Fine, I'll prove it to you. Your husband's name is Mike Sei. He has two moles on his left butt cheek, and a big birthmark on his right thigh. His favorite position is doggy style, and—"

Serena hung up. Her mother and father would be disappointed—no, devastated—if she got divorced. Her successful marriage to a doctor had been paramount evidence to them that they raised her right. Serena glared at the large wedding picture in the living room. In it, she had been made up and Photoshopped to look flawless, thinner, and taller. In the picture both she and Mike smiled with the daft happiness of newlyweds. Serena wanted to tell every smiling bride in the world that it was all an illusion, a lie, that marriages don't last, or at least the love doesn't, even if the marriage survives.

The phone rang again. She let the answering machine pick it up.

"Hi, this is Mike, I'll be at the hospital all night. There's a last minute operation and no other surgeon could do it, so I have to step in. Don't wait up. Bye."

Tears spilled from her eyes. Of exactly what nature was this "operation" of his? But what could she do, ambush him at the hospital? What would be the point of that?

Serena walked back to the washing machine and moved the load into the dryer, separating out jeans and shirts to hang up on the balcony later. She clutched her sad, lavender sweater to her chest. She identified with the poor, ruined thing now and could not bring herself to throw it away.

Serena spent the night tossing and turning between nightmares. In one dream, flames were devouring everything in her apartment with her in it. Everything went dark and hot as the fire engulfed her. In another dream, she was at a charity event where her husband was being auctioned off. The auctioneer rattled off numbers quickly, like a fast-speaking commercial spokesperson. Attractive women, some younger than her, some older, raised their paddles and continuously outbid Serena, until she realized that she could not afford to keep her husband. The bidding went as high as five million.

The next morning, when Serena woke up, Mike was still not home. She took a shower and went to school. She didn't teach until three in the afternoon, but she did not want to run into Mike. She had a lot of student workbooks to grade, anyway. At noon, she and Ms. Lai, a home economics teacher, went downstairs to buy bentos from the cafeteria. They ate across from each other at their desks in the shared teacher's office, a giant rectangular space which housed over eighty desks, one for each instructor.

"You look tired," Ms. Lai said.

"Yeah, I couldn't sleep last night." Serena rubbed her temples.

"It's been so cold these few days, I'm having trouble sleeping, too. My circulation is very bad, and my feet are always freezing, even if I wear socks," Ms. Lai said. "It's lucky that you have a husband to warm your bed."

Ms. Lai blushed a little when she talked about husbands and beds, but Serena frowned. She was about to say something when she heard her name.

"Teacher Sei? You have a visitor," an elderly math teacher called from across the room.

Serena put her chopsticks down in her barely-touched bento and pushed back her chair.

At the door stood an attractive woman in a delicate silk chiffon dress, a sparkling necklace of diamonds around her neck. She looked oddly familiar, but Serena could not place her. The math teacher self-consciously touched his bald spot in front of such an attractive visitor.

"Hello." Serena extended one hand toward the woman.

The woman shook her hand with a claw-like grasp, scraping Serena's palm with her jeweled, acrylic-tipped nails, and said in a raspy voice, "Can we talk somewhere more private? It's about my son."

"Sure," Serena said, "If you don't mind, we can sit on the benches by the basketball court."

"I have a better idea. Let me treat you to lunch. Do you have class later today?"

"Not until three. But—"

"Please. It's for my son. It's important, and I need your professional advice," the woman said.

Serena thought it very odd that the mother of a student would need her advice, of all the teachers at the school. As a music teacher, she hardly spent any individual time with students, unless they were in the school band and needed extra help. Maybe this was band-related. Or about applying to music school. There was something about the woman's demeanor that intrigued Serena. She nodded.

At a cozy Western-style restaurant on Fushing South Road, Serena sipped black tea with lemon while the student's mother ordered sizzling-steak meal specials for both of them, complete with soup, salad, and dessert.

"So what is it you wanted to talk about? And your son's name is?" Serena asked.

"To be frank with you, Mrs. Sei, my son isn't born yet," the woman said.

"Pardon?"

"I am pregnant. It's a boy. I wanted to talk to you today about him," the woman said.

"Why me?" Serena asked. It occurred to her that the woman might be insane.

"Because you are married to my son's father," the woman said with a smile showing all of her pearly teeth.

"What?"

Serena pushed her chair back and was about to stand up, but the woman reached across the table, put her hand over Serena's, and pressed the tips of her acrylic nails into the back of Serena's hand.

"There's no need to make a scene. You are already here. I'm not toying with you, or trying to make things difficult," she said.

"Let go of my hand," Serena hissed.

"Have you seen the variety show *Beautiful Lady*?" the woman asked.

That was why the woman looked so familiar—she was on TV! She was Jenna Lee, the host of a small-time variety show about makeup and fashion. How did her husband meet someone in the entertainment industry, someone who so ostentatiously wore tacky jewels all over her nails and neck? And she was *pregnant*? Serena sank back into her seat, the world spinning around her.

"I guess you recognize me now. So you see, if you make a scene, it will be all over the news. I'm pretty sure the guy at the table over there is paparazzi. Please stay and eat. Listen to my business proposal. I come to you with sincerity."

"What do you want from me?" Serena asked through her teeth.

"I told you over the phone. I would like to offer you five million NT in cash, in exchange for you to divorce your husband. That's over a hundred and eighty thousand US dollars. You could buy real estate in America and live there if you want to. I can even arrange for someone to help you get a green card. What do you make as a music teacher at a middle school? Thirty thousand NT a year? I think five million is a very good deal for you."

"My husband is not for sale."

"I am really doing this for all of our sakes. I want my son to grow up with a father. I don't mind if the media jumps all over me for being an unwed mother, but the child is innocent. I don't want people to call him a bastard or look down on him."

Serena looked away.

"Think about it," Jenna continued. "You don't have anything to lose and have everything to gain by accepting my offer. You aren't tied down with a child, so you can still marry someone else. Maybe have a child of your own."

A waitress arrived with two bowls of creamy corn chowder and ornately plated fresh salads that looked like volcanoes exploding with alfalfa sprouts. The green leaves of the sprouts, shaped like hearts, laughed in Serena's face. Her appetite for both men and food had gone. The issue of not having children had always been a thorn in her side. It was no secret her husband's parents thought there was something wrong with her, because she had been married for five years and had not yet reproduced. And now, to have a trashy entertainer with loads of cash rub it in her face . . .

Meanwhile, Jenna Lee picked up her salad and dumped it into her soup, scraping the plate with her nails. She swirled her salad and soup mixture together and spooned a mound of the mixture into her bright red mouth. Serena felt disgusted by the way the woman ate. Who puts salad into soup?

"I'm so hungry. I hope you don't mind if I dig in. I'm eating for two." Jenna spoke with her mouth full.

Serena thought to herself that Jenna Lee, ex-model though she was, looked like a cow, literally, with those green sprouts coming out of her mouth.

"I am leaving now. The answer is still no." Serena stood.

"Think about it. Between a divorce settlement and the five million, you'd be the richest middle school music teacher ever! Why live the way you do when you can be rich and free?"

Serena picked up her purse and walked out.

When she got home that night, Mike was cooking dumplings in the kitchen. He'd forgotten to turn on the exhaust fan and the kitchen was filled with steam and the smell of boiled pork and starch.

"I came home early," he said. "I am making dinner."

"I'm not hungry."

"I take it she spoke to you." Mike stirred the dumplings.

"I can't believe you have the nerve to stand there and ask me about it." She pictured for a moment dumping the entire pot of scalding liquid and dumplings all over her cheating husband.

"I really didn't mean for this to happen."

"How did you meet her?"

"There was a benefit event for the hospital. She made a large donation and was honored as a VIP guest. The chief of medicine sent me to the banquet in his place to accept her check, take a picture, and say thank you on the hospital's be-half," he said.

"And?"

"That's how we met, that's all."

"How long has it been? When did you find out she is pregnant?" Serena closed her eyes since she could no longer look at him.

"Since last December, but she only just told me she was pregnant. I was surprised."

When Serena finally looked at Mike, she saw in his eyes and the wavering corners of his mouth that he was actually happy that woman was pregnant, and she hated him for it. She knew he wanted a child, but to have one from a mistress was going too far.

"How could you do this to me?" she asked, trembling. "For five years, I've made your meals, cleaned your house, done your laundry, shared your bed, waited for you to come home at night. And you run off with a cheap entertainer?"

"She said she would offer you enough money to make it worth your . . . while. She is very wealthy. And of course, I would give you a very generous alimony and share of assets in the divorce, on top of whatever she offers you."

"Don't you mention divorce to me!" Serena cried. "Or money! Nobody, nothing around here, is for sale!"

"Please consider it, Serena."

Serena entered the master bedroom and slammed the door.

During the next few days, Jenna Lee's photo was all over the tabloids and entertainment news. She had gone public about her pregnancy and leaked Mike's name and the hospital he worked at. Jenna even told reporters about the five million NT offer she made to Serena, except she embellished the story from her own point of view. The newspapers portrayed Mrs. Sei as a crazy shrew who pushed her husband into the arms of another—more loving and now expecting—woman. Reporters swarmed like wasps: at Mike's hospital, outside Serena's school. The principal temporarily excused her from her teaching duties to keep the scandal and paparazzi as far away from the school as possible. The phone rang incessantly; reporters wanted Mr. or Mrs. Sei to make a statement or do an exclusive interview. Finally, the answering machine, beeping miserably, rejected all calls: "Sorry, the message box is full."

Even while hiding at home, Serena could not turn on the TV without hearing about Jenna Lee.

"Eighty-five percent of our viewers online say that the wife is a fool for not taking the money. Let's see what viewers in the streets of Taipei say," a female reporter was saying.

"Men are pigs. She should take her five million and move on," a young woman said before smiling and making a victory pose with two fingers for the camera.

"There is a child involved. Children must always be considered first. The wife should think about the innocent child." This middle-aged male interviewee spoke emphatically, gesticulating with both hands.

Serena turned off the television and dashed the remote control onto the hardwood floor. It cracked open and spewed out two AA batteries.

He is *my* husband, she thought to herself, *mine*. Nobody can make me divorce him, and nobody can make me let him go. She found a stick of lipstick from her purse and took it to the wedding picture in the living room. *Wo de*, MINE, she wrote, in two large red characters, onto the glass. She went to other picture frames displayed around the house and scribbled over each of them, *wo de, wo de, wo de*. Then she moved on to the walls.

Seven Pieces at a Time

At Tai Ping Junior High, my classmates nicknamed me *Pih*, Fart. That's probably the reason I never went to senior high school. And not finishing school is why, from the age of fifteen, I worked full-time in my parents' corner store in the middle of Shi Ling Night Market. Everybody thinks I'm retarded or something, but the truth is I simply don't know what to say a lot of the time. I can think perfectly fine, but when I speak, the words don't come out entirely right. A speech impediment would probably be a more correct thing to call my condition, but people don't care. They just like to think I am stupid.

Working at my parents' store is how I met Natasha. She has golden hair and the kind of face you see in a Western magazine, all angles and sharp lines. I could never pronounce her name, so she let me call her Na Na. It's a good name because there are Chinese words for it, *there there*, so soothing and soft, and because I gave the name to her. Soon she went by "Na Na" all the time, she said, because it's easier for people to say. I'm a little mad that she used the name that I gave her with other people—that takes the specialness away a bit.

Na Na used to come to the store two or three times a week. She bought the same thing every time: one pack of green Wrigley's gum with seven pieces in it. She'd take the gum from the rack and place a ten-NT coin on the counter, and I'd give her three one-NT coins for change. She must have a whole jar of one-NT coins, I used to think to myself, since she never gave me smaller change, always ten-NT. Once I showed her a value pack of Wrigley's gum, because she bought so much every week it would save her money to just buy a larger pack, but she smiled and pushed the value pack away; she only wanted seven pieces at a time. She pointed at the weekly calendar on the counter and flipped pages. Each time she flipped a page, she made a shrugging motion. Then she let all the pages fall back into place and pointed at the current week, making a thumbs-up motion. I thought about that for weeks, for months. I decided it was a good philosophy. Instead of being greedy and hoarding a lot of gum, possibly risking losing it or letting it go stale, you can get it seven pieces at a time, just like life. You consider everything one week at a time like the weather report and never worry beyond that because there's no point. You might die next week, and somebody else will eat your extra gum.

I would never say that to my son, of course. I don't say much to my son. He's only one, and he can't walk yet. I figure he's too young for the depressing realities of life. He's confused enough as it is. Na Na speaks Russian to him, my parents and I speak Taiwanese or Chinese to him, and he never responds. He has no words. He has some sort of speech delay, my parents say. I asked them if I had speech delay when I was little and they said absolutely not, I started speaking earlier than most kids. Something must have happened along the way. The teasing didn't help. You see, I hardly spoke to anyone at school, but once, just once, I farted out loud during siesta time. Since then my name has been Fart. My classmates said I farted more than I spoke because I farted instead of talking. I hope nobody makes fun of my son in the future, call him names like *bai chi*, white idiot. His name is Bai, white, because that's my favorite color, and also Na Na's favorite color—at least I think it is.

I ran into one of my old junior high classmates the other day. She couldn't believe that I was married and had a son. *You, Fart, married? A son?* It was mean of her to still call me Fart after all those years. If I see her walking down the street next time, I will close the door and pretend the store is closed. I don't want my son to hear her call me Fart. I am a father, and a father should keep his dignity in front of his son. To your son, you are always someone big, someone important, not a fart or a joke. If you set a bad example and lose face before your children, the children will grow up with low self-esteem and become the running dogs of gangsters or accept beatings from their spouses. I learned that much from TV.

Na Na worked in a bar. She was one of those Russian white girls who came to Taipei to dance in bars for money. She wasn't really a prostitute. Though I think she had probably slept with a customer or two that she liked, but she was too quick-tempered to "service" just any man. A sex worker? Forget it. She would never go down on her knees and put her mouth around a stranger's dick—she was too proud. She didn't even do it for me. She did like to dance for them, though. I didn't understand why a man would need a woman to perform a dance for him, but I didn't mind too much. She was tall, like a goddess made of white chocolate, and she liked to show off her body because it was such an overwhelming sight, so gorgeous and creamy, like a marble statue. There was a crease here or there and her breasts sagged a little bit, but she carried herself very nicely. She was almost as tall as me, and I'm pretty tall for Taiwanese, 182 centimeters. Bai will be tall when he grows up, I'm sure. Unless he gets bullied too much at school and becomes depressed and covered in acne, and turns to drugs, alcohol and smoking, all of which will stunt his growth. Otherwise, he will be tall, light-skinned and handsome. White and Asian are a good mix, and he's a nice-looking kid: long lashes, big eyes, and everything. He looks like a Russian child with dark hair, although I'm not really sure what a Russian child looks like. I can only imagine a very short and chubby Na Na.

I lost my virginity to Na Na on our first date; at least, I like to call it our first date. She took me by the hand and led me to her one-bedroom apartment down the alley from my store. She kicked the front door shut, unzipped my pants, stared at my privates, jerked me off, and laughed because I came so quickly. Her apartment was small, essentially a bedroom with a corner paneled out for a bathroom. Later, I noticed there was no stove. All she had to cook with was a hot water kettle to make instant noodles. After jerking me off, she wiped my softening dick off with a rough towel covered with dark stains. She removed the rest of my clothes. She examined every part of me, touching my chest over and over again. I've heard that white women like Asian men because our bodies are smooth; maybe that was what she was thinking. As her hands moved down toward my privates, my dick grew hard again.

And just like that, she sat on me, and took me all the way into her amazing, slippery body. It felt so good and warm and wet inside. It was the most wonderful thing in the world. I couldn't stop after that; it was like drugs. She screamed things in Russian. I had no idea what she was saying, but I could tell she liked it. We had sex all night. Na Na didn't go to work the next day, and I didn't go home. When our stomachs were both growling, I went out and bought some *yang chun* noodles from a food stand nearby. We wolfed down the noodles in hot soup, and fell asleep in each other's arms. Soon I woke up with an erection and drove it into her, and we became animals again.

A few months later, when Na Na pointed at her stomach, slightly fuller than it used to be, and made cooing baby noises for me, I understood she was having a baby. She also pointed at me. I unwrapped a piece of gum, rolled it into the shape of a ring, and put it on her long, bony ring finger. She smiled. That was how we were married. We were never officially married because there was something wrong with Na Na's papers—that was as much as I understood, after one of her Russian friends tried to translate for me in her bad Chinese. It was okay. I loved her, she loved me, and we were going to have a little baby. I began referring to her as my wife in front of everybody. My parents liked the idea of me being married and having a kid. They were living in the countryside by then, having moved into my grandmother's house after her death.

Na Na stopped going to work after her stomach became too obvious. Her breasts were more magnificent than ever, like helium balloons fully inflated. She stayed in her apartment and slept all day or sat with me in the store, reading Russian novels and chewing a lot of Wrigley gum. She still only wanted the seven pack gum, even if she could finish two packs in a day. It was a good thing she agreed not to smoke during her pregnancy.

Bai was a gigantic, healthy baby. Na Na screamed like I had never made her scream when Bai came out of her. When I leaned close to her during labor she slapped me, yelling something in Russian. I took her hand and squeezed it, but she looked away. I offered her gum, which she grabbed and tossed straight across the room. The obstetrician chuckled at me.

"It's the hormones and the pain. The bad mood will pass."

I stared at Bai. He was plump and adorable. When I put my face close to his, one of his hands reached out and hit me with curled fingers.

"Good reflex," the doctor said.

He was wrong, however, about Na Na's bad mood. It did not pass. He instructed us not to have sex for six weeks after the baby, so I stayed away from her, but that made her even angrier. She grabbed my dick, forcing it hard and drawing me close to her all the time, but I had to say no and push her away. Sometimes she got mad and left the apartment. She couldn't go back to work yet because her tummy still looked pregnant, so I don't know where she went when she ran out like that. When six weeks finally passed, and I wanted to sleep with her, she just slapped me and ignored me and pitched the TV remote control at my head.

Some days she only chewed gum and didn't eat. She also smoked a lot of cigarettes. She lost the baby weight quickly and went back to work. Na Na wasn't always around to breastfeed Bai so he got used to formula, which he sucked down eagerly and grew plump on. My parents came and helped me take care of Bai. He was a very easy baby. He didn't throw tantrums and could sleep through anything. Just change his diaper, give him a bottle, burp him, and put him in the crib. This was all stuff I could do between counting out change for customers at the store.

One night, Na Na came home very drunk. Her floral dress was unbuttoned at the top so her breasts were mostly exposed. She threw things at me, and when I tried to stop her because she was waking Bai, she hit me. Having taken taekwondo for self defense in all of my middle school years, I blocked all the blows, which made her even angrier. We fought and struggled until she was tired, and then her mood changed. She reached for my pants and unzipped them. At first I thought she was going to hurt me down there, but instead she started stroking my dick and sucking it. I unbuttoned her dress and fucked her hard, the way she liked it. We fell asleep together, exhausted.

The next night, Na Na didn't come home. I waited all day the next day. When I closed the store, she still wasn't home. She had left for work like usual the previous night, taking only her purse with her. The closet was still full of her clothes. I went to the bar she worked at and asked her friends and boss about her, but they said that she didn't come to work and they hadn't seen her or heard her say anything about leaving.

A month later, I got a small envelope in the mail with a foreign postmark on it. I tore open the flap and shook the contents out of the envelope. It was a small package of Wrigley gum. It had seven pieces in it. I understood her meaning completely. Na Na really was living life seven pieces at a time, and my seven pieces with her were up. I looked at Bai, who toddled over and grabbed the bright green gum packet from me. He held it up to his nose and smelled it.

"Mama?" he asked, one of his first words. I didn't know he remembered Na Na and the gum she was always chewing. Maybe he remembered the gum on her breath, or her ripping open the bright green packaging.

"Yes, from Mama. For you, Bai."

Crisp Skin Thick Soup

THE ONLY THING I have from home is a jade necklace that my mother gave me. I come from a small Vietnamese village, *My Lai*, where we had a small rice field on which we relied for a living. The river gave us water and a modest harvest. Two harvest seasons ago, Mother died giving birth to a baby brother, a silent infant who never lived to see the sun rise. Father took to the bottle, stopped working the fields, and our growing debt was like a balloon filling with air, ready to burst. Every store I went to, I had to owe money or give them something in return. Some of our neighbors tried to help me plant the rice sprouts I'd gotten on credit, but Father, drunk on cheap rice wine, waved a rusty sickle at them, threatening to kill anyone who meddled in our business.

When young men in our village asked for my hand in marriage, he scared them all away. "Anyone who touches my daughter will die."

I was only sixteen and wanted more. I ran away.

My childhood friend Han gave me a lift to Saigon on his new scooter and introduced me to his friend's cousin, a big-deal business lady, Mrs. Rie, who worked in the city. She was the wife of a man who owned a special agency, a company that introduced Vietnamese girls to foreigners as brides. I had no money, couldn't even pay the matchmaking fee, but Mrs. Rie persuaded her husband to let me owe it to them until I was successfully married to a foreign client.

She looked me up and down. "You're not especially beautiful, legs too thick and hips too narrow, face all bones, but I think someone will like you."

They showed pictures they had taken of me, dolled up with make-up and swathed in elegant clothing, to their clients, and in three weeks, they had sealed my marriage with a Taiwanese man.

"But I don't speak Taiwanese."

"Everybody speaks Chinese there, my dear. Plus he will not mind, I guarantee you." Mrs. Rie smiled, nice to me all of a sudden now that I was bringing them business. "He's looking for a wife, not a conversation partner. Just smile and look pretty and cook and clean."

She was pleased that the Taiwanese man was willing to pay nearly half as much as an American would have for a Vietnamese bride. I never saw any of that money, of course. It all went to the agency and they even claimed I owed them many fees for the arrangement as well as rent for the time I slept in the cockroach-ridden warehouse they kept me in, so in the end I got little more than a coin purse of pocket money.

My new husband met me at the Chiang Kai-shek International Airport. He was holding a sign with my name written in English: Lei Lee. My last name would be changed soon. My husband was Mr. Ting, and I was to become Lei Ting.

All the buildings in Taipei are so tall and shiny, the people so happy, that it is strange to me. Their faces are Chinese faces, not terribly different from us Vietnamese, maybe a little coarser, broader, yet their lives the exact opposite. Here, rice comes from burlap bags in supermarkets, not the fields. I don't know where the fields are here.

My husband, a retired soldier, has a bearded chin that scrapes my skin when we kiss, hollow eyes I am afraid of meeting, and thinning, gray hair. We communicate with a few words of Chinese at first, mostly gesturing. I prefer nighttime, when no language is necessary. He gives me little medicine pills to swallow, draws an X with his fingers, and makes the shape of a woman's round belly on me. He does not want me to become pregnant, and these pills will protect me.

We live on the eleventh floor of a residential building. Our apartment has just one bedroom and is smaller than our old hut in Vietnam, but I like it here because it is clean and has large windows to let the sun shine in, just like the outdoors back home, except with air conditioning.

The strange thing is that there is no source of fire in his apartment, no stove, nothing to cook with. His dinner comes from the night market: an oyster omelet from a food stand, along with rice, vegetables, and fish from a cafeteria. He shows me the way twice, and soon it is my job every night to buy his omelet and some cafeteria food for both of us.

From nine-to-three every weekday he sweeps and mops the floor in a public library nearby while I go to the morning market, take a walk in the neighborhood, clean the house, or watch Taiwanese television at home. We have Japanese cable channels, but I prefer local soap operas. I learn a lot of Chinese from them. I especially like the period shows where all the characters wear traditional Chinese clothing, flowing robes embellished with sashes, wide sleeves that flutter. I would have liked to wear those clothes. But, I still wear my plain blue gowns that begin at the jade necklace around my neck and end at my ankles, even in the hot Taiwanese summer. It is important for me to still feel like I am Vietnamese, because even if I married a Taiwanese man, it does not change me inside; I am still Lei Lee. I will not forget my ancestors, and it is important to honor them.

As I venture out more during the day, I make friends. Most of them are maids and nannies from Vietnam. If given a choice, one always picks their own. My companions tell me the latest gossip. One woman, Taiyun, has a neighbor who got a mail-order bride from Russia. Russia! She has skin the color of milk and porcelain. White women are idolized goddesses in Asia.

"How can you possibly buy a white woman?" I ask.

Taiyun smiles slyly and makes the motion of rustling money in her right hand.

"Lots and lots of money. And do you know what, that man's family treats her as if she were a princess instead of a mail-order bride—no offense, Lei Lee."

"What do you mean?"

"They are afraid that she will be bored, so they find little kids to be her English students, even though her English is so bad that I would laugh at it. But they don't care, they think she is so wonderful to marry their son. Rich people, of course. They're just nutty. And they can't wait till she gives them little mixed, foreign looking babies, beautiful and creamy-skinned."

"Well, I certainly wouldn't want to teach English, I don't envy her that," I say.

"The point is, they try so hard to please her," Taiyun says. "From what I can tell, your husband treats you like my employer treats me. Like a servant. Because they bought us— they know it and we know it."

"Well, I don't think of it that way. I want to please my husband because if he is happy then I will be happy because he will be good to me."

"Right, right," Taiyun scoffs. "You are perfect material for a mail-order bride. Exactly what he ordered."

"That's not a very nice thing to say."

"Let me ask you, if you go out to buy his dinner in the night market and come back, say, twenty minutes later than usual, will he be mad?"

"Maybe, if he is hungry. Once I walked a little slow, and—"

"Ah ha! That's exactly what I mean. He treats you like a servant. A man will not scold his wife like a child for being late. He would only scold a servant."

I don't say anything. Half of me sees Taiyun as being jealous of my legal status as a wife here, my freedom to stay in Taiwan as long as I like without having to work on a temporary contract or bribe officials for a visa. The other half of me understands Taiyun perfectly. Mr. Ting feels that I'm something he owns, someone he can order around. Indeed, I cannot even think of him in my mind as Hsia, which is his name—to me he's always Mr. Ting. My friends are used to it and no longer laugh at me for calling my own husband by the title Mr., but I still feel embarrassed and confused about who he is to me. My companion? Lover? Master?

I am still thinking of what Taiyun said today as I leave the house to get dinner.

It's a fifteen-minute walk to the omelet stand, where a long queue winds to the left, pushed back by the passing crowd. The owner notices me and nods. I come daily, and today he's in a good mood. He gestures to the cook to give him the next omelet, catches it in a styrofoam container as the cook tosses it to him, and with a swift flick with his ladle, drizzles coral-colored, tangy sauce all over it. I hand him five ten-NT coins and he gives me the container in a little red-and-white striped plastic bag.

"Just one, not two?" He winks first one, then his other eye. "Buy one get one free, only for you, number one customer."

He knows I am buying Mr. Ting's omelet. He also knows I am a Vietnamese mail-order bride, and leers. I wave my hand *no* and walk away as politely as possible.

I think oyster omelets are disgusting, and overpriced. I ask Mr. Ting why he will not get a stove, so I can cook all this food for less money than we are paying the vendor and cafeteria owner.

"Can you make *o ah jian* just like the stand? Eh? What about the flavor of the special sauce?"

"I could learn."

"Forget it. I don't want the smell of cooking in my home," he says. "It is a small space, and I won't have it smelling of grease and oysters. Just go buy the food and stop questioning your husband."

I feel the heavy ring of keys in my pocket as I drag my feet in plastic sandals through the night market. Because of moments like this, that come back to me over and over again, when he ends the conversation with scolding me, the resentment wells up. But I vent it in small ways, little by little, so that I can still like him. Sometimes I spit in his coffee in the morning, or into the special sauce on the omelet.

Recently, I stopped taking the little pills. Even if Mr. Ting doesn't want a child, I want a son, a boy whom I could love, one who would grow up to be tall and strong and who would take care of me. I don't believe that a man would really not want a child once it is here—doesn't every man want a boy, a small version of himself? It will make him feel manly, to have produced another human being, especially in Mr. Ting's case—he is forty-five years old already—what does he have to look forward to besides family? When I am pregnant, I'm sure Mr. Ting will change his mind and love the child. It's only human nature.

At the cafeteria, the *lao ban nian*, female owner of the store, smiles and nods when I come in. She works hard and is polite to all customers, adult or children, mail-order brides or not. As she hands me two paper containers for the food and a plastic bag for steamed rice, I open my mouth to speak, which surprises her because she has probably never heard me talk before. She must have thought I did not speak Chinese.

"Can I have *su pi nong tan*?" *Su pi nong tan*, crisp skin thick soup, is a creamy Western-style soup cooked in a soup tureen with a layer of golden puffed pastry baked on top. It would be the ultimate luxury to taste; I could imagine the buttery flakes of pastry contrasting with the rich texture of the soup. I would eat it so eagerly my tongue and the roof of my mouth would burn, but it would be worth it. Several days ago, I watched an episode of a food channel show about gourmet restaurant dishes that featured the soup, and could not stop thinking about it since.

"Why, sure, of course you can have some soup!" She smiles broadly. She is happy for more business, especially since *su pi nong tan* is not cheap, one hundred NT per bowl.

"But it is too hot for you to carry home. You see, the soup bowl is baked in the oven."

I think about this. "It's okay, I will eat it here."

The *lao ban nian* smiles and calls to her chef, a short, handsome man who looks half Taiwanese, half some kind of Caucasian. "One *su pi* soup!" Then she turns to me courteously. "Please have a seat and wait here."

"I'll get the food first," I say and walk toward the steaming trays of green, brown, and yellow dishes shiny with grease.

I pay her in advance, handing over two crumpled bills.

"Are you sure it is okay if you make Mr. Ting wait?" She looks at me with concern. Why is a stranger worried about me being scolded by my own husband? Is it so obvious?

I nod. I want the soup.

Besides, it's too late to back out. I've paid for the soup and am all ready to eat it.

The chef seems to be taking his time. The *lao ban nian* turns to me at the table and apologizes every few minutes. "Sometimes the oven is slow to heat up," she explains. I smile and say that it is no problem.

The handsome chef finally comes out with my beautiful soup, the rounded pastry top domed like a breast, golden and perfect, a few black sesame seeds sprinkled over the top. He holds it with oven mittens and an extra rag. The *lao ban nian* rushes to put a coaster down before me as he sets the bowl down.

"Enjoy," she says. "And be careful, it's very hot!"

I look at my *su pi nong tan*. I can hardly bear to break the beautiful, crisp skin at the top, but I do. My husband is waiting for food at home, and probably grumbling already. I make a small hole in the pastry skin, which breaks immediately and some buttery pieces crumble into the soup. Steam rises from the hole in the puff pastry, and I smell the fragrance of creamy mushrooms and chicken. I make a larger hole with my spoon and reach into the soup, picking up a small piece of pastry, moistened with creamy soup, that had fallen in. I blow on it to cool it down, then put it in my mouth. Delicious. I savor every bit of my soup, blowing on each spoonful but still burning my mouth. I'm sweating though it is winter and unseasonably cold; the soup warms and satisfies me. It may sound ridiculous, but this is one of the best moments of my life. I feel free, like I am defying the universe by sitting here, enjoying *su pi nong tan* as my husband waits hungrily at home for his dinner.

I want to linger in the store longer, enjoying my *su pi nong tan*, but there is no more. Not one scrap of mushroom remains at the bottom of the bowl. I smile at the owner on my way out.

During my walk home, some men look at me. They see my red cheeks and red lips from the soup; they must think I am in love. I turn my gaze to the ground and walk as quickly as possible. After all that waiting, the omelet must be only lukewarm.

When I open the door, Mr. Ting is standing right behind it.

"Where were you?" he asks.

"In the night market," I reply.

"Why were you so late?"

"I just . . . walked more slowly."

"You are forty minutes late and you say you walked more slowly? What kind of lie is that, what were you up to?" He raises his voice.

"Nothing." I walk past him to put the food on the counter.

"Don't evade my questions like that."

He feels more and more free to scold me in Chinese since he knows I understand it well enough now. He seems angrier than is appropriate for my being late, though, even if he is hungry and worried.

"I'm sorry. Here, let's eat now." I use my most soothing voice.

"After you explain this." He holds something out in front of me. It is a blue-and-white foil and plastic container with twenty-one little pills in it. He found the contraceptive pills I did not take in my underwear drawer.

"I . . . I forgot all about them," I stammer, sensing his anger.

"Forgot? You lying woman, how dare you lie to me twice in so short a time, did you forget I bought you from your country, gave you a good life and home here, you ungrateful wench! How dare you disobey and deceive me?"

I move back toward the door as he advances. I suddenly remember that he used to be a soldier and that my mother had warned me to stay away from soldiers. So many of them were damaged, she said, and they were not balanced people, often prone to violence.

"I'm sorry, I'm sorry—" I say over and over again.

"Sorry is not enough. Where have you been? Have you been sleeping with someone else? The cafeteria cook, that mixed bastard? Do you want his child, is that why you are not taking the pills?"

"No, no!"

I reach for the door, but he slams it shut. He is strong, and much bigger than me. He uses his left arm to twist me around, yanks me closer by my jade necklace, and lands a punch in my abdomen with his right fist. The pain is sudden and fierce. I feel a snap and the little jade beads fall to the floor, scattering in different directions. I scramble around on the floor, trying to gather them up, but they roll away from my trembling fingers. He grabs my upper arm, pulls me up and punches my stomach again.

Tears stream down my face as I struggle to breathe. I feel my consciousness leaving me but I hold on tight to the few beads in my hands. The pain is like a screw in my body, screwing tighter and tighter. The last thing I think of is that if I wasn't a mail-order bride this would not be happening to me. If I was Taiwanese, like him, he could not feel so much more superior, or if I were a Russian mail-order bride, then I would be tall, strong, and beat him right back. With the last strength I have, I lunge toward him with the beads closed in my fists and try to punch him in the abdomen, as he had done me, but it takes him only a slap to land me on the floor again. The last beads escape from me and I curl up into a C shape, groaning. I can feel warmth and wetness down there, the blood coming from inside. He lunges and lands on me, but I kick him in a vital place, and it is his turn to land on the floor.

I open the door and run out, into the street. I do not know where I can go, but I know I must run, and keep running.

Daughter

L IN TOOK THE MRT to and from work every Tuesday and
Thursday between Liu Zanli and Da Zi stations, during
the worst part of rush hour. Not only did she never have
a seat, she was constantly pushed around, stabbed by the
corners of studious students' open textbooks, old women's
umbrellas, and old men's canes. Lin clasped her pink handbag close to her in case any of the pushers and pokers were
also pickpockets. Her handbag always had a small stack of
thousand-NT bills in it because Lin didn't believe in credit
cards. She didn't even have a bank account until Da Zi Middle School hired her and insisted that her salary had to be
wired to a post office savings account rather than honoring
her request of receiving it in the form of cash in an envelope.

Lin taught home economics and art at Da Zi Middle
School. Strictly speaking, she was a sculptor, but the school
wanted her to teach drawing and sewing. So, she showed
students how to do double stitches, single stitches, and
hems, and ordered cheap cotton fabric so students could
make aprons for their semester-long projects. She told her
art students to bring 2B pencils, soft erasers, and gave them

sketching paper on which to sketch each other in pairs. On nice days, she sent them out to draw in the sun, in whatever medium they chose—watercolor, gouache, charcoal, colored pencil, oil pastels. She watched them from under a tree, a food magazine in her lap. Lin rarely commented on student projects, and everybody received an A at the end of the semester. What kind of home economics or art teacher would give a student anything but an A in a competitive Taipei middle school? If a teacher of such unimportant subjects brought down students' overall grade point averages, the students would revolt and beat her up on her way from school to the MRT station.

Lin took long baths at night and had a membership to the twenty-four-hour movie rental store next to her building, which allowed her to check out unlimited films each month. Lin's parents were remarkably old (mother forty-nine, father sixty-three) when they had her, an only child, and by now, long dead (breast cancer, lung cancer). When they were still alive and their minds were not yet silenced by cancer cells, they had encouraged Lin's artistic career. Unfortunately, they died before her first opening in Taipei Professional Art Academy's North Wing. It was an installation—lots of space, with tiny papier-mâché animals strung in white necklaces from the ceiling, and clay animals stacked together. Regardless of species, the clay animals were equal in size—the rats as large as the rhinos, the giraffes as tall as the Chinese sparrowhawk. The central concept of the piece, titled "Under, On Top Of," had to do with proliferating cancer cells, food chains, and human impact on the environment.

Lin's artistic career never went anywhere after she started teaching at the age of twenty-three. She played with clay, still, but since there was nowhere to unload her art and her apartment and studio were getting too full—she cut down on the sculpting. She took up cooking creatively, collecting challenging recipes from gourmet magazines, and arranging food with expert color-coordination and composition on the plate. She often felt it a shame that she had to consume her culinary masterpieces, which sometimes seemed more beautiful than her best sculpture of all—a large bunny rabbit as tall as her, with lifelike fur and perpetually-alert ears. That rabbit cost her thousands of NT in clay yet now sat gathering dust in a corner of her studio, by the north window. She thought she saw a crack in the large bunny the other day, but couldn't bear to look close enough to confirm. A colony of smaller clay bunnies clustered quietly around the king-sized bunny like its subjects. At some point Lin gave up all other figures and concentrated on bunnies. It was some time after her parents' death, about the time that her professors at National Taiwan University of Arts stopped encouraging her to send her slides out to galleries and grad schools and residencies. Lin did not mind. She got a stable teaching job and that was more than most of her poor, more talented classmates had.

Lin never bothered to date, either. She was neither ugly nor beautiful, just plain, and a little too tall for the preference of most Taiwanese men, generally short themselves. Some might consider Lin plump, progressively so over the years, at least by Taiwanese standards. She had long, straight hair, the hairstyle that required the least amount of maintenance other than shampooing twice a week. Lin demonstrated in the past twenty or so years of her life that it was possible for a marriageable, healthy woman living in Taipei City to avoid most human contact and potential suitors by not socializing at all and not talking to colleagues except when absolutely necessary.

Lin was forty-three and regretted nothing in her life. She did not want to change her days, her routines—long baths, irregular but fancy homemade meals, unlimited rental movies, and the occasional satisfaction one got from sculpting a furry clay bunny.

Lin was thinking about a movie she saw last night as she stood in the crowded MRT, hugging her purse. She hadn't understood the movie, mostly because she was confused which man was which woman's husband and which woman was which man's girlfriend. There was some swapping going on, and the tall, Caucasian actors lost Lin within the first half hour. Lin decided she would watch the film again tonight, before returning it. If she still couldn't understand the relationships the second time she watched it, carefully reading the subtitles and trying her best to memorize the actors' faces and relationships with one another, she would give up.

The train was especially crowded today. The door opened and closed at Taipei Train Station, the busiest transfer station where three MRT lines converged, and people flooded into Lin's compartment so that the passengers were all pressing against and touching one another. People in the MRT car did not enjoy this forced physical contact with strangers, but precisely because the other passengers were strangers, it was okay to pretend not to notice the touching of arms and elbows and occasionally, hips. Lin felt a push on her back that nearly made her bump her head into a pole, but she was too tired to turn around and glare at the offender. The doors closed, nearly catching a young woman's curly tresses. The woman yelped and pulled her bleached and permed hair with fraying split ends to the front of her right shoulder, then spent two minutes inspecting it and smoothing it out, as if comforting a baby. Lin watched her for a while with a blank expression on her face. She never understood the vain young women with over-processed hair, expensively styled yet horrible haircuts, painful-looking high heels, and tight clothing. Didn't their feet hurt? Didn't they feel cold? Did they really think anyone cared? Lin certainly didn't.

The MRT car pushed into motion, creating a whooshing noise that grew more high-pitched as the car accelerated. Lin closed her eyes. She felt some shifting and squeezing around and about her, which was common because some people couldn't balance themselves well enough on a moving MRT car and felt the need to lean on other people in order not to fall. At any rate, the space was so tight that passengers' bodies kept other passengers' bodies pinned in an upright position, so that no one would ever fall all the way to the floor. There was simply no space.

Suddenly, Lin became conscious of something pressing against her left ass cheek through her linen pants. She shifted a little to avoid being touched by whatever it was, but the bag, or briefcase, or cane, or umbrella, followed her behind persistently. She turned her head to see what it was, and saw a short little man with a weasel's face. The weasel's fly was down and his dick was pressed against the fabric of her pants. It was the size of a small walnut—uncircumcised, wrinkled, and disgusting. Lin wanted to scream but didn't want everybody else in the car to think she was crazy. They couldn't see what was going on, and as far as they were concerned, she was the crazy one. She wanted to pull the red M-shaped lever that would stop the MRT train, but she didn't want to be in the six o'clock news—"Hysterical Middle School Art Teacher Waylays Rush-Hour MRT Traffic." Lin could not move. She had violent fantasies about the little man with his tiny, wrinkled penis, scenes she had seen in movies applied directly to him: the man's head lopped off by an axe, his body parts separated and ground-up by machines and made into fresh steamed dumplings, or multiple bullets hitting his body, *bang bang bang bang bang*, the blood saturating his green T-shirt and beat-up jeans. She wanted to hit him, but at the same time she didn't want to touch him.

The next minute seemed to last longer than all the years Lin spent teaching at Da Zi Middle School. She had never felt so humiliated, violated, and dirty. Had she kept to herself, protected herself from human contact and men and all of that, only to be insulted by a horrible little man with a wrinkled walnut for a penis?

The car pulled into the next station, Si To, not her station. Lin rushed out. The weasel followed her out. They held on to each other's presence with their eyes amidst the people pushing to enter the MRT car and the passengers struggling to get out. When the crowd cleared between them and only Lin and the weasel were left, Lin exploded into tears and profanity, words she had only learned from movies, words she never used or ever thought of using until now. She hit the man with her pink handbag, cursing and screaming and crying. She no longer cared if she was making a scene. She continued to hit him while he ducked and covered his head with his hands, trying to shield himself from the much taller and larger woman's blows. The pair moved across the lobby of Si To station in this manner. Finally, when they were close to the exit, the little man ran out the door, and Lin sat down on the dirty plastic bench beside the entrance with a thump. She sobbed heartily into her hands. At least she did not touch him, not even once, though she would have to throw out the sullied handbag when she got home.

Nobody would understand and nobody cared. Why hadn't she made some friends? Who would she tell, who would she talk to? If she had married at some point, perhaps her husband would have picked her up in a modest yet serviceable car today after school, and the weasel would not have put his dick up against her butt cheek and she wouldn't have had to chase him all the way out of the station, hitting him like a crazy bag lady, which no doubt everybody in Si To Station thought she was.

As Lin convulsed and choked on her sobs, she felt someone tapping her on the back. A police officer? She turned and was surprised to see a little old woman's wrinkled, sunken face.

"I saw what happened," the old woman said slowly. She had no teeth and her mouth puckered in each time she uttered a consonant.

"I saw what happened, and I am so glad that you went after him. You are a brave girl," the old woman said.

An old man came toward Lin and the old woman.

"My wife and I saw everything," the old man said, gesturing toward the old woman to indicate that she was his companion.

"You did the right thing. I wanted to hit him, too. You are brave. Don't cry," the old man said.

The old couple nodded earnestly at Lin.

Some middle-aged women were looking at them, and the old woman held up her raisined hands and addressed them. "This is a brave girl. A dirty man insulted her and she fought back."

The middle-aged women nodded sympathetically all around. The expressions on their faces said, *Good for you.*

Lin's tears dried slowly on her burning cheeks, and through her tears she nodded at the elderly couple to express her gratitude. The old woman put her wrinkled hand on top of Lin's.

"Don't cry, daughter," she said.

Lin swallowed a lump in her throat. These old people could have been her parents. In this moment, they were. Lin was grateful, and for the first time in many years, she felt her heart opening.

My Strange Grandpa

I GUESS I wasn't all that surprised when my mother told me that Grandpa's caretaker, the Indonesian maid, had run away. As horrified as we were that a girl willing to leave her country for the purpose of making money was not willing to take care of Grandpa in exchange for good wages and room and board, we also felt vindicated. It seemed to excuse us for all our complaints about Grandpa.

My grandpa has been living with us for as long as I can remember, since Grandma died. I heard that when I was little and he wasn't as senile, things weren't so bad, but honestly, for as long as I can recall, Grandpa has been something of a skeleton in the closet for my family.

He's like any other eighty-something-year-old grandfather, except he's exceptionally demanding, even for a Taiwanese elder, and worst of all, he watches the Japanese porn channel at a high volume all day in his room. When I was in elementary school, I asked my mother if I could bring some friends home, but she always suggested that we go to McDonald's or the park instead; she even went as far as giving me three hundred NT just to make sure we would entertain ourselves outside the house.

"It's not good to disturb your grandfather," she said in a troubled tone.

"I don't think Grandpa minds," I said, thinking she was mean, but pocketing the money anyway.

Now, of course, the reason we couldn't have my little girlfriends over was because my mother didn't want my classmates to hear the weird noises coming out of Grandpa's room. I didn't know what they were at the time, and was actually more or less used to them. I'd accidentally seen him watching it a few times, just Japanese people being dramatic about taking baths together—they were often not dressed, so that's how I understood it.

When I was in third grade, Grandpa tried to explain to me where babies came from. He brought me to his room, where he had the Japanese channel playing, and told me about the different parts on a boy and a girl and how they fit together when the boy is excited. My mother interrupted, knocking on the sliding Japanese doors.

"Lille, are you in there? Father, have you seen Lille?"

"I'm in here, Mom," I called back. "Grandpa's teaching me about sex."

I said this, not quite understanding everything, though I had at least been able to learn the word "sex." My mother rushed in, grabbed me by the arm, and pulled me with her all the way to the kitchen.

"Forget what your grandpa said. He's really old, and sometimes old people say strange things," she said, stuffing an orange into my hands.

I ate the orange and soon forgot about it, although whenever I passed Grandpa's room and heard the wailing or moaning noises, I wondered if it had something to do with sex. In fifth grade, I finally learned in health class how sex worked and understood exactly what Grandpa was watching hour after hour day to day. I asked my mom why nobody never at least requested that Grandpa lower the volume on the television, or just quit watching it.

"It's too embarrassing," she said. "Your father won't have anything to do with it. Nobody wants to mention to him that we know what he's watching. And we don't know how he will respond. He may think we are making him lose face."

"But he's your father," I said.

"You can complain to him if you want," she said, flailing her arms.

I didn't.

Grandpa got worse—not in terms of health, since he was always in fantastic health, but his behavior. He watched porn more and more often, sometimes in the middle of the night, and took to calling my mother or me into his room to massage his back every hour of the day.

Of course we love him and want to take care of him, but sometimes it just gets to be too much. I started taking part-time jobs in senior high just to stay away from home longer, and the last year of senior high, while I was spending all my waking hours preparing for the difficult Joint College Entrance Exam, I took the bus to a cram school directly after class, then went to the library to study until closing time at 10:30 p.m. In some ways, I should credit my grandpa for helping me get into the best teachers' college possible, Shida. I tried so hard to stay away from home that I had to spend my free time studying until I was a Chinese, geography, history, math, earth science, English, and Taiwanese Constitution whiz.

The summer I took the Joint College Entrance Exam and found out that I was accepted to attend Shida, we finally found Grandpa a caretaker, an Indonesian girl. We told people we had gotten a caretaker because I was going away to college and my mom would need someone else to help take care of Grandpa.

The hiring agency said the girl they were sending us was smart and capable, although only eighteen years old, with a junior high school education. In the few weeks of her training in Taiwan, they told us, she had already learned some basic conversational Chinese and sufficient nursing skills that would allow her to take care of an elderly person. Grandpa had a wheelchair that he used sometimes, but he didn't need diaper changes or special assistance, so when we applied with the agency, we were at the bottom of the list according to medical needs. Luckily, my mother sped up the process by accepting a caretaker with the minimum level of qualifications. Just as well; the hardest things she had to do were deal with pornographic sound effects and being woken up at random times at night to massage Grandpa. For that matter, she'd probably be ordered to massage him nonstop during the day, too.

Things started out alright. The Indonesian girl, Gem, had big, round eyes, a round face, and cute smile. She had the regulation haircut that a lot of Indonesian agencies forced their workers to get: a short, cropped boy's haircut. She was kind of pretty, and that made Grandpa happy, at least for the first few hours. Then he remembered that everybody was supposed to be at his service.

"Listen to me," he announced, "all of you have to obey my orders, especially you, Gem. You have to learn to massage me properly."

My mother wanted to confirm that Gem knew the word massage, so she walked over to Grandpa, and started rubbing his shoulders in slow motion and saying the words *ma sa ji*, horse kill chicken, Chinese for "massage."

Gem nodded and repeated, "Horse kill chicken" and moved toward Grandpa. Grandpa looked back at her and pointed at his shoulders, indicating for her to begin immediately. Then we taught Gem how to help Grandpa in and out of his wheelchair. My mother still bought the groceries from the grocery store, but sometimes Gem accompanied her in the kitchen while she cooked—that is, until she got called away by Grandpa.

Over the next few weeks, I witnessed in Gem's young face all the psychological stages of a new employee, from initial excitement to disillusionment. The first few hours with us, Gem was eager to please, polite, bowing and nodding and smiling at everyone. By the first week, she had seen the porn, experienced the round-the-clock massage requests, and seemed slightly disappointed by the circumstances of her work. After week two, she had no expression on her face, and I thought I saw her clenching her teeth while massaging Grandpa.

My mom and I didn't really talk to her that much, first of all because her Chinese was still poor, and also because, in a way, we were worried she would complain to us. The whole reason we hired someone to take care of Grandpa was because we didn't want to deal with him and his needs. With Gem taking care of him, we were free to leave the house and not feel guilty, to be in the house and not be on massage duty 24/7. We gave Gem a nice bedroom with a single mattress, chest of drawers, desk, mirror, and chairs, and on top of that paid her extremely well, the higher end of her hiring agency's specified range of salaries, despite her limited qualifications.

Unfortunately, good pay and a room of her own weren't enough.

When I returned to my dorm after biology class this afternoon, I saw a missed call from my mother on my cell phone.

"Lille, you won't believe this," she said in a low voice when I called her back.

I couldn't tell what was going on. Perhaps a relative that she disliked had a knocked-up daughter, something unfortunate yet juicy at the same time. "What's up, Ma?"

"I think Gem ran away."

"What?"

"I thought I heard someone leave the house kind of late last night, but I didn't check to see. I never saw Gem this morning, and her room is still empty. I just called her agency. The woman I spoke to apologized and said they would send us someone else as soon as they can."

"Send us someone else? What does that mean?"

"She didn't say much, just that Gem told them she wanted a three-day vacation to meet her boyfriend and the agency said no, and then she said she wanted a reassignment and they said no again. I'm not quite sure I understood all of it, it sounded kind of complicated, but anyways, the conclusion is Gem's going back to Indonesia."

"I don't understand why she asked her agency. She could have asked you and Dad to let her leave for three days if that's what she wanted."

"That's why I'm confused. Maybe the woman at the agency made up the boyfriend story to make us feel better about her wanting to leave our home."

"So we can't get her back?"

"No, I asked that, too, and they were very firm about that. They basically told me we would never see Gem again."

"That's very odd. Makes it sound like we were abusing her," I said.

"So, anyways, I put Grandpa on the waitlist for another caretaker. He's throwing a fit right now, hollering for his cute little Indonesian masseuse."

Mom lowered her voice even more. "You know, it's strange to think that your grandpa, the way he is now, was my father, the man I looked up to as a kid. He was very strict and proper. You would think he and your grandma had never had sex. They never touched each other, and he didn't touch us," she said.

"So how is it now he watches porn with the volume all the way up and asks people to massage him all day?"

"I think maybe when you're very old, your body and mind make you pay for all the things you denied them before. All the instincts and needs you neglected, they come back to haunt you so you can never be satisfied, and you begin acting out."

"Mom, you're being very morbid and strange. All this pressure with the caretaker and Grandpa must be getting to you. Do you want me to come back this week? I can skip my Friday classes and stay for the weekend."

"It's okay. I just wanted to talk, and ask you something. Do you think I'm going to end up like your grandpa?"

"Mom, you're fine! Grandpa is just old and dotty. And I think, on a certain level, he simply doesn't care anymore. Old people are so respected. They can do whatever they want and order everybody around. So, some of them do."

"I hope that's all it is," my mom said, and I could hear in the background my grandpa calling first for the Indonesian girl, then for my mom to massage him.

"I have to go. I'll see you this weekend." She hung up.

I sat down on my bunk bed with my biology textbook in my lap. I thought about my poor, frazzled mom, my dad who turns a deaf ear to everything going on about him, and the mystery of the runaway Indonesian girl. I wonder what my dead grandmother, whom I've never met, would have thought of all this, and of my strange grandpa.

Discussion Questions

1. In "The Strange Objects Museum," how does Sheri change as the story develops? What leads to these changes?

2. In "Yuan Zu Socializing," why does the protagonist call her actions a form of revenge?

3. Discuss Brian's rejection of Sonnie in "Lock, Stock and Two Smoking Barrels."

4. What might wearing a bra symbolize to Lily in "And Then There Were None"?

5. Is the narrator in "Betel Nut Beauty" reliable? Why do you think she withholds information from the reader for most of the story?

6. How do Chinese beliefs around a "red suicide" inform your interpretation of how "Writing on the Basement Wall" ends?

7. In "Simple as That," how do gender and culture inform Jolie and Mike's relationship?

8. Consider the conflicting roles of the narrator in "Immersion": graduate student versus "PR girl." How are they compatible or incompatible?

9. In "Passport Baby," why do you think Lin Lin stole the baby? Was this foreshadowed in the story?

10. If you were Serena in "Mine," would you accept Jenna Lee's offer? Why or why not?

Biographical Note

Born and raised in Taipei, Taiwan, Yu-Han (Eugenia) Chao received her BA in Foreign Languages and Literatures from National Taiwan University and her MFA in fiction from Penn State University. The Backwaters Press published her poetry book, *We Grow Old: Fifty-Three Love Poems*, and Another New Calligraphy, Dancing Girl Press, and BOAAT Press published her chapbooks. Her website is www.yuhanchao.com, and she maintains a blog about nursing and writing at yuhanchao.blogspot.com. She currently lives in California, where she works as a registered nurse and educator.